BIG HORSESHOES TO FILL

Licensed By:

IDW @IDWpublishing
IDWpublishing.com

COVER ARTIST:
Amy Mebberson

SERIES EDITORS:
Jonathan Manning and Riley Farmer

COLLECTION EDITOR:
Alonzo Simon

COLLECTION DESIGNER:
Johanna Nattalie

COLLECTION GROUP EDITOR:
Kris Simon

978-1-68405-952-2 26 25 24 23 1 2 3 4

MY LITTLE PONY, VOLUME 1: BIG HORSESHOES TO FILL. MARCH 2023. FIRST PRINTING.

Originally published as MY LITTLE PONY issues #1–5.

Special thanks to Hasbro's Ed Lane, Tayla Reo, and Michael Kelly for their invaluable assistance.

For international rights, contact licensing@idwpublishing.com.

"The Case of the Missing Unity Crystal"

WRITTEN BY
Celeste Bronfman

ART BY
Amy Mebberson

"Puff-Sitting"

STORY & ART BY
Robin Easter

"Pipp Gets Really Real"

WRITTEN BY
Mary Kenney

ART BY
Trish Forstner

"Lightning Rod and the Mirror of Mayhem"

WRITTEN BY
Casey Gilly

ART BY
Abby Bulmer

Colors by
Heather Breckel

Letters by
Neil Uyetake

The Case of the Missing Unity Crystal

art by Amy Mebberson

ANYTHING TO REPORT, EXPLORER?
I THOUGHT I SAW THE ROYAL CASTLE, BUT IT WAS JUST A STACK OF ORANGES AT THE MARKET.
CANTERLOT MIGHT BE A BIT TOO FAR FOR US TO SEE FROM HERE. BUT YOU'LL FIND IT ONE DAY.
YOU THINK SO?
"TWILIGHT SPARKLE BUILT THE GATE OF THE ANCIENTS TO WELCOME THOSE WHO BELIEVED AND TRUSTED IN THE MAGIC OF FRIENDSHIP TO CANTERLOT."
YOU LEAD WITH LOVE, SUNNY.
AND SO LONG AS YOU MAKE SURE NO EARTH PONY, PEGASUS, OR UNICORN EVER FEELS LESSER THAN BECAUSE OF WHO THEY ARE, CANTERLOT WILL ALWAYS BE YOUR HOME.
NOTHING NEW TO REPORT, DAD. BUT NOT EVERY WEEK CAN BE AS EVENTFUL AS REUNITING THE UNITY CRYSTALS AND RESTORING MAGIC TO ALL PONYKIND.
DO YOU THINK TWILIGHT WOULD BE PROUD OF ME?

OF COURSE SHE WOULD BE! AND THE PIPPSQUEAKS AGREE. SAY HI!
LIVE

IF YOU'RE DONE LIVESTREAMING, WE'VE GOT A GAME OF FLYBALL TO PLAY!

THE RULES ARE SIMPLE. GET THE BALL IN THE NET FIVE TIMES, AND YOU WIN. BUT THERE'S TONS OF STRATEGY TO THIS GAME AS WELL.

OOH, ARE WE PLAYING A GAME? IS THIS A PIE-EATING CONTEST? A CAKE-EATING CONTEST? A COOKIE-EATING CONTEST?

NO NEED TO TWIST MY HOOF, I'M IN! POINT ME TO THE FIELD.

IT'S UP NEAR THAT CLOUD OVER THERE...

OH! WELL, I ALWAYS SAY IT'S JUST AS MUCH FUN CHEERING ON YOUR FRIENDS AS IT IS PLAYING WITH THEM...
SEE YOU LATER, IZZY!

?
OVER HERE!

THESE CRITTERS SAY WE'RE GETTING CLOSE.
I CAN FEEL IT.

WHAT ARE WE LOOKING FOR?
A FAMILY OF BUTTERFILLIES. BUT THEY SCARE EASY SO WE'VE GOT TO KEEP VERY QUIET.
SO NO SPEAKING.
VEEERRRRY QUIET.
HE SAID NO SPEAKING. YOU HEAR THAT, EVERYPONY?
!

!!
!
!

GUESS EVEN THE BUTTERFILLIES HEARD THAT.

A RAINBOW SWIRL. AND MAKE IT A DOUBLE.

SHE SWERVES, AND SHE SCORES!

HOLD IT STEADY.
IZZI
IT'S MY MAGIC. IT'S--
!?

I GOTCHU,
I GOTCHU!
HELP.
SOMEPONY
HELP ME!
I'M
COMING!
WHAT
THE--
I'VE GOT
YOU.
BUT...
PIPP!

COME ON, COME ON!
BELIEVE YOU CAN FLY, AND YOU WILL!
THAT'S YOUR PLAN B?!
OKAY... MOVING ON TO PLAN C.
BINGO!

ZOOM
SBAKK!

SPLOOSH!

SPLOT!

WHAT'S THAT, CLOUDPUFF?
YOU WANT ME TO KNOW PIPP'S NO LONGER FALLING THROUGH THE AIR AND IN IMMINENT DANGER?
WISH YOU COULD HAVE FIGURED OUT A WAY THAT WASN'T SO STICKY.
STICKY... OR DELICIOUS?

IT WAS SO FREAKY. ONE SECOND, MY WINGS WERE TOTALLY FINE, AND THE NEXT MY MAGIC STARTS GLITCHING OUT.
THE SAME THING HAPPENED TO ME.
AND ME.

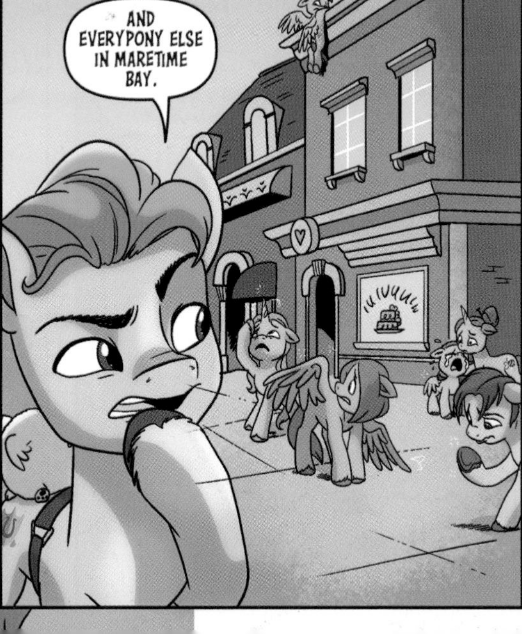
AND EVERYPONY ELSE IN MARETIME BAY.

EXCEPT FOR SUNNY. YOUR WINGS WORKED THE WHOLE TIME.
I COULD STILL FEEL MY MAGIC GLITCHING. BUT IT SEEMS BETTER NOW.
OH, LOOK, MY MAGIC'S COMING BACK, TOO! LOOKS LIKE THIS TOPSY-TURVY MAGICAL CRISIS HAS BEEN AVERTED!
JUST BECAUSE OUR MAGIC'S BACK DOESN'T MEAN IT'S **BACK** BACK. IF IT FIZZLED AWAY ONCE, THE SAME THING COULD HAPPEN AGAIN.
AND NEXT TIME WE MIGHT NOT HAVE A SMOOTHIE MACHINE AT THE READY.
NONE OF THIS MAKES ANY SENSE. SO LONG AS THERE'S UNITY BETWEEN OUR SPECIES, THE CRYSTALS ARE SUPPOSED TO KEEP OUR MAGIC STABLE.
PEGASI, UNICORNS, AND EARTH PONIES HAVE NEVER BEEN TIGHTER. IF ANYTHING, OUR MAGIC SHOULD BE STRONGER.

YOU'RE RIGHT. SO IF MAGIC IS GOING HAYWIRE, IT CAN'T BE ABOUT FRIENDSHIPS-- OH NO.
DO WE THINK THAT'S A GOOD "OH NO" OR...?

AND WE'RE RUNNING.
HAVEN'T I BEEN THROUGH ENOUGH TRAUMA FOR ONE DAY?
GET YOUR HOOVES MOVING, PIPP!

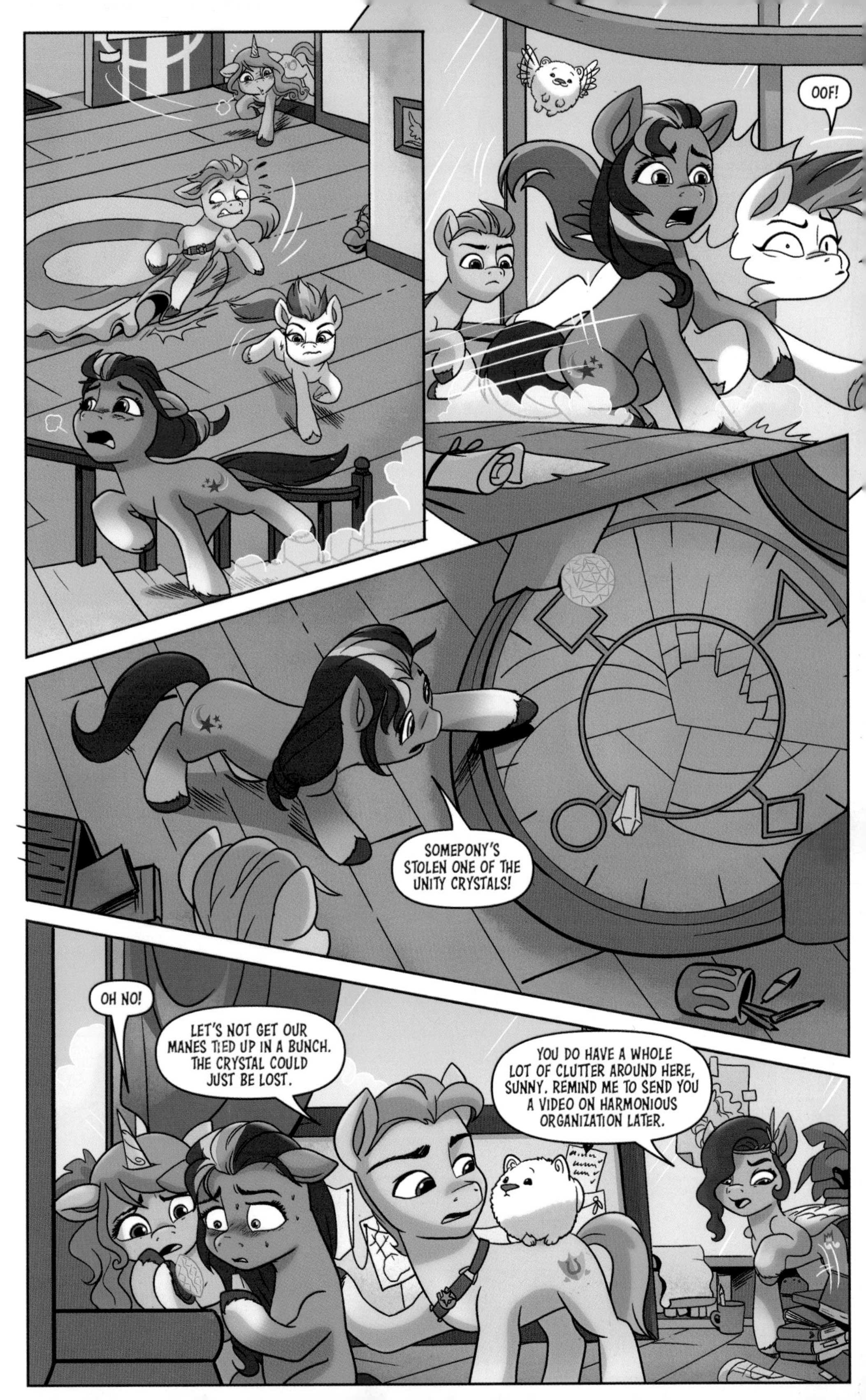
OOF!
SOMEPONY'S STOLEN ONE OF THE UNITY CRYSTALS!
OH NO!
LET'S NOT GET OUR MANES TIED UP IN A BUNCH. THE CRYSTAL COULD JUST BE LOST.
YOU DO HAVE A WHOLE LOT OF CLUTTER AROUND HERE, SUNNY. REMIND ME TO SEND YOU A VIDEO ON HARMONIOUS ORGANIZATION LATER.

I DIDN'T THINK THE CRYSTALS COULD BE SEPARATED. THIS LOOKS INTENTIONAL.
THESE CRYSTALS ARE A SYMBOL OF PONYKIND'S ABILITY TO LIVE IN HARMONY.
IF SOMEPONY SEPARATED THEM, IT'S BECAUSE THEY WANT MAGIC TO FIZZLE OUT UNTIL IT'S GONE--FOR LIFE TO GO BACK TO THE WAY IT WAS BEFORE.
BUT WE ARE NOT GOING TO LET THAT HAPPEN.
WE WERE ABLE TO UNITE THE CRYSTALS ONCE BEFORE. WE CAN DO IT AGAIN. LET'S FIND THE CRYSTAL THIEF AND GET THAT CRYSTAL BACK!
YEAH!
BAK! BAK! BAK! BAK!
MISSION. INITIATED.

PIPPSQUEAKS, I KNOW YOU'RE ALL SCARED RIGHT NOW... AND YOU SHOULD BE!
YOUR MAGIC MIGHT BE BACK, BUT IT WILL DISAPPEAR AGAIN, AND THEN COME BACK, AND THEN DISAPPEAR AGAIN, UNTIL IT DISAPPEARS COMPLETELY... BECAUSE SOMEPONY STOLE A UNITY CRYSTAL.
IT'S. REALLY. BAD.
HEY! THEY DESERVE THE TRUTH.
AND A BIT OF HOPE. ALL YOU'RE DOING IS THROWING THEM INTO PANIC MODE.
MY PIPPSQUEAKS MEDITATE WHEN THEY'RE OVERWHELMED. THEY DON'T PANIC.
IF MAGIC'S GOING TO DISAPPEAR, I'LL FLY AS MUCH AS I CAN NOW!
WHAT IF IT FIZZLES OUT WHILE YOU'RE IN THE AIR? *WHAT THEN?*
I CAN'T GO BACK TO MANUALLY BRUSHING MY MANE LIKE SOME PEDESTRIAN PONY!

NOPONY SHOULD BE SCARED BECAUSE WE ARE GOING TO SOLVE THIS BY BEGINNING OUR SEARCH RIGHT HERE, WHERE THE BREAK-IN HAPPENED.
AND THAT'S THE THING ABOUT BREAK-INS...
notebook stash!

...NO MATTER HOW HARD A THIEF TRIES, THEY'LL NEVER BE ABLE TO LEAVE THE SCENE EXACTLY AS THEY FOUND IT.
SOMETHING'S ALWAYS JUST A LITTLE BIT OFF. A LITTLE BIT BROKEN... IN.
OOH, I WOULD LIKE FIFTY OF THOSE HATS PLEASE. WHERE'S IT FROM?
PROBABLY ALL THIS CLUTTER.

DETECTIVE ZIPP ALWAYS COMES PREPARED.
DETECTIVE ZIPP?
THAT'S RIGHT. BECAUSE I ZIPP MY WAY THROUGH A GOOD MYSTERY UNTIL I TRACK DOWN THE PERPETRATOR AND BRING THEM TO JUSTICE.
WE'RE GOING TO GET THOSE CRYSTALS BACK IN NO TIME!
I WOULDN'T BE SO SURE. HOW MANY SUCCESSFUL CASES HAVE YOU SOLVED, DETECTIVE ZIPP?
WELL... THIS WOULD TECHNICALLY BE MY FIRST CASE. WHICH, IF YOU THINK ABOUT IT, MEANS I'VE NEVER HAD ANY UNSUCCESSFUL CASES EITHER!
SO IF YOU'RE READY, LET'S GET SOLVING.

PIPP FILMED THIS BEFORE WE LEFT THIS MORNING. AND AS YOU CAN SEE FROM THE RAINBOW LIGHT SHINING BEHIND HER, THE CRYSTAL HADN'T BEEN STOLEN YET.
LOOK CLOSELY. WHAT ELSE DO YOU SEE?
TO CATCH OUR THIEF AND FIND OUR MISSING CRYSTAL, IT'S IMPORTANT TO KEEP AN EYE OUT FOR THE SPECIFICS. THE MINUTIA. THE DETAILS.
BESIDES THE GORGEOUS WAY THE LIGHT'S BRUSHING MY CHEEKS?
YEAH, BESIDES THAT.
THE VASE HAS BEEN MOVED.
ZOOM
CONSIDER THE CASE ZIPPED.

IT DOESN'T LOOK LIKE IT BELONGS TO ANYPONY I KNOW.
IT'S LONG AND STRETCHY LIKE THE FUR OF A PLATIPONY OR A UNICOOGER! OR MAYBE EVEN A PUGASUS!
IF WE FOLLOW THE SCENT, WE'LL FIND THEM.
YOU UP TO THE TASK, CLOUDPUFF?
WOOF!
NO, IT'S THE CRYSTAL THAT WAS STOLEN. IF I'D BEEN STOLEN, I WOULDN'T BE HERE RIGHT NOW.
GO ON. GET A GOOD OL' SNIFF OF THIS.
!
BUT I HAVEN'T PACKED MY BAGS! IF I GO A MORNING WITHOUT MY MEDITATION PILLOW, AROMATHERAPY CANDLES, TONER, AND MOISTURIZER, I WILL BE A NERVOUS WRECK WITH BLEMISHES. THAT'S A BAD COMBINATION.
WE'VE GOT A HIT. LET'S ROLL.
BAK BAK BAK
CLOUDPUFF COULD LOSE THE SCENT IF WE DON'T LEAVE NOW!
C'MON, SIS. IT'LL BE FUN.

SEVERAL HOURS LATER...
YOU'LL LET ME KNOW WHEN WE HIT THE FUN PART, RIGHT?

THE GOOD NEWS IS THAT WHOEVERPONY STOLE THE CRYSTAL MUST BE GETTING JUST AS TIRED.

HERE'S THE DEAL, PIPPSQUEAKS. WE'VE BEEN TRACKING OUR THIEF FOR A MILLENNIUM--
THREE HOURS.

BECAUSE ZIPP IS A HORRIBLE DETECTIVE, HITCH KEEPS ATTRACTING ALL THESE CREEPY ANIMALS, IZZY KEEPS SINGING, AND CLOUDPUFF KEEPS GOING IN CIRCLES! SO IF YOU'RE HEARING THIS, FOR THE LOVE OF ALL PONYKIND, SEND HELP.
!
NO, MY PHONE DIED! AND I DON'T HAVE A CHARGER BECAUSE SOMEPONY DIDN'T GIVE ME ENOUGH TIME TO ***PACK ANYTHING.***

WE WERE GOING TO LOSE THE TRAIL AND MAYBE LOSE MAGIC ALTOGETHER! I THINK THAT'S MORE IMPORTANT THAN A PHONE CHARGER--
NOW I CAN'T EVEN CALL FOR HELP IF WE NEED IT!
I KNOW YOU'RE ALL SCARED. I AM TOO. BUT WE CAN'T LET FEAR TEAR US APART. THE ONLY WAY THROUGH THIS IS BY STICKING TOGETHER.
YEAH, FINE.
WHATEVER.
YOU WERE RIGHT ABOUT ONE THING, PIPP--EMPHASIS ON ONE THING. FOLLOWING CLOUDPUFF ISN'T GETTING US ANYWHERE.

WE'LL GET A BETTER LAY OF THE LAND FROM ABOVE THE TREES. ZIPP, PIPP, CAN YOU FLY?

WINGS SEEM TO BE WORKING RIGHT NOW.
AND IF THEY STOP WORKING IN THE AIR?
WE'LL MAKE SURE WE'RE LOW ENOUGH THAT THE TREES CAN CATCH OUR FALL.
I CAN ASK SOME OF THE CRITTERS AROUND HERE IF THEY'VE SEEN ANYTHING.
I DON'T THINK IT'S A GOOD IDEA TO SPLIT UP.
WE DON'T HAVE A CHOICE. EVERY MINUTE THAT CRYSTAL IS SEPARATED FROM THE OTHERS, OUR MAGIC WILL GLITCH OUT MORE AND MORE.
WE NEED TO USE EVERY ADVANTAGE WE HAVE. THAT MEANS USING OUR MAGIC.
I STILL THINK--
--WELL THAT'S OKAY!
I'LL JUST LOOK FOR A PLACE TO USE MY MAGIC DOWN HERE, OKAY?!
LEAVE IT TO ME!

A FEW HOURS LATER...
IT'S A GOOD THING THEY LEFT ME DOWN HERE... TOTALLY GOOD!
I MEAN, WHO ELSE WOULD'VE NOTICED THIS TOTALLY NOT-SUSPICIOUS CAVE IN A TOTALLY NOT-SUSPICIOUS PART OF THIS TOTALLY NOT-SUSPICIOUS WOOD?
AND WHO ELSE COULD'VE... MOVED.
ALL.
THESE.
RRROOOCCKKS?!
HELLOOOO, CRYSTAL THIEF. I COME IN PEACE AND WITH A SONG IF YOU'D LIKE TO HEAR IT!
?
OOPS!
CLANG!

CRYSTAL THIEF, IF THAT'S YOU, I'M SORRY FOR HITTING YOU WITH A ROCK.
WHOA...
IS THIS A CREEPY GATE FOR A CREEPY CRYSTAL THIEF? BET I CAN'T SAY THAT FIVE TIMES FAST.

A CREEPY GATE FOR A CREEPY CRYSTAL THIEF, A CREEPY GATE FOR A CREEPY CRYSTAL THIEF, A CREEPY GATE--
ELCOME TO CANTERLO
CANTERLOT?!

I SPY, WITH MY PONY EYE... **ANOTHER** LEAFY TREE.
OOH, THEY'RE ALREADY BEGINNING TO SHED. THAT'S GOING TO INCREASE THE EFFECTIVENESS OF POLLINATION AND HELP THEM FLOWER.
IF I FALL RIGHT NOW, IT'S **NOT** BECAUSE MY MAGIC GLITCHED OUT. IT'S BECAUSE YOU'RE PUTTING ME TO SLEEP.

THE TREES ARE WAY TOO THICK FOR THE CRYSTAL THIEF TO HAVE GOTTEN THIS FAR ANYWAY.
WE SHOULD REGROUP WITH THE OTHERS. SEE IF THEY FOUND ANYTHING.

DOWN HERE!
HITCH!

WHERE'S IZZY?
I'VE BEEN CALLING OUT TO HER. SHE SHOULD BE HERE SOON.

WHAT'S GOT INTO YOU, BUD?

AS SOON AS YOU LEFT, CLOUDPUFF RACED OFF. I THOUGHT HE WAS RUNNING TOWARD SOMETHING BUT TURNS OUT HE WAS RUNNING AWAY--

--FROM THIS!

THE DOOR'S OPEN. BET WE'LL FIND THE CRYSTAL THIEF THROUGH HERE! HOW'S THAT FOR DETECTIVE WORK?

THE SACRED *GATE OF THE ANCIENTS!*

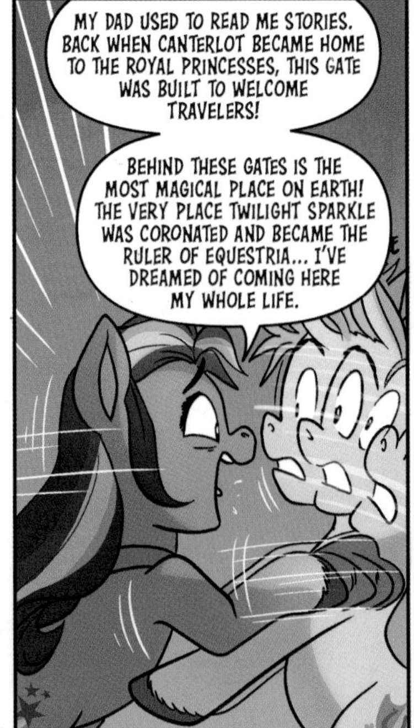
MY DAD USED TO READ ME STORIES. BACK WHEN CANTERLOT BECAME HOME TO THE ROYAL PRINCESSES, THIS GATE WAS BUILT TO WELCOME TRAVELERS!
BEHIND THESE GATES IS THE MOST MAGICAL PLACE ON EARTH! THE VERY PLACE TWILIGHT SPARKLE WAS CORONATED AND BECAME THE RULER OF EQUESTRIA... I'VE DREAMED OF COMING HERE MY WHOLE LIFE.

I MADE IT, DAD.
PAT PAT

YIKES. YOU DREAMED OF COMING HERE? NO OFFENSE, BUT IF THE THIEF NEEDED ENOUGH MONEY TO MOVE OUT OF THIS GHOST TOWN, MAYBE WE SHOULD LET THEM KEEP THE CRYSTAL.
COME BACK
NOPONY'S LIVED IN CANTERLOT FOR A WHILE. BUT I PROMISE YOU'LL ALL BE ABLE TO FEEL THE MAGIC ONCE WE START EXPLORING!
UH... SHOULDN'T WE WAIT FOR IZZY?
EVERY ONE OF THESE SHOPS IS A RELIC FROM THE PAST. CANTERLOT CULTURE LIVED HERE!
!!!
THE CRYSTAL THIEF.

THE TRICK WITH THESE THINGS IS ALWAYS TO TAKE THE THIEF BY SURPRISE. SO KEEP QUIET AND FOLLOW MY LEAD.
CLOSED

YOU'VE BEEN CAUGHT RED-HOOFED, CRYSTAL THIEF! GIVE US BACK THE PEGASUS CRYSTAL!

YOU MADE IT!
Specials
IZZY?

HOW LONG HAVE YOU BEEN HERE? WHY DIDN'T YOU CALL US?
I TRIED, BUT YOU FLEW TOO FAR AWAY. SO I CAME HERE TO LOOK FOR THE THIEF MYSELF!
WE'VE GOTTA TRY THESE DONUTS. THEY'VE BEEN AGED, LIKE, A HUNDRED YEARS, WHICH MEANS THEY'RE REALLY FANCY!
IT'S NOT LIKE CHEESE, IZZY. IF YOU EAT THAT, YOU'LL BE SICK FOR DAYS.
WELL, WE'RE NOT GOING TO FIND OUR CRYSTAL THIEF HERE. LOOKS LIKE WE'LL HAVE TO DO SOME EXPLORING AFTER ALL.
YES!
I ACTUALLY WILL HAVE THIS DONUT.
HEY!
I CAN'T BELIEVE I'M HERE...
I THINK YOU CAN BELIEVE IT, AND THAT'S SORT OF THE PROBLEM.
I ALWAYS SAW CANTERLOT AS THIS PERFECT BEACON OF FRIENDSHIP. A PLACE WHERE UNICORNS, EARTH PONIES, AND PEGASI LIVED IN HARMONY AND NOPONY EVER FELT LEFT BEHIND.
THAT'S WHAT YOU WANTED TO CREATE IN MARETIME BAY.
YEAH. BUT SEEING CANTERLOT LIKE THIS...
...MAKES ME QUESTION HOW HARD IT WOULD BE TO KEEP IT THAT WAY.

HEY, PONIES!
LISTEN UP. ACCORDING TO NEW EVIDENCE THAT'S JUST COME TO LIGHT, IF WE WANT TO FIND THE CRYSTAL THIEF, I BELIEVE WE NEED TO HEAD TO THE ROYAL CASTLE.
THE ROYAL CASTLE!
YOU'RE A GENIUS, ZIPP! YOU KNOW THE THIEF MUST BE SOMEPONY WITH A POWER COMPLEX WHO WOULD BE DRAWN TO THE CASTLE.
THEY WOULD ALSO HAVE THE BEST VIEW FROM UP THERE TO SPOT INCOMING THREATS!
YEAH... OF COURSE I REALIZED ALL THAT...
...AND ALSO, I MIGHT HAVE SEEN THE DOOR BEING OPENED.
GET INTO FORMATION, EVERYPONY. WE'VE GOT A THIEF TO CATCH!

I'VE GOT THE DOOR!

COME ON, LITTLE HORN-HORN. YOU CAN DO IT!

MAGIC'S GONE AGAIN.

PUT YOUR HOOVES INTO IT!

CLICK!
PRINCESSES CELESTIA, LUNA, AND TWILIGHT SPARKLE ALL STEPPED HOOVES EXACTLY WHERE I'M STEPPING! EEEE!

HISTORY HAS BEEN MADE IN THIS THRONE ROOM A THOUSAND TIMES OVER... AND IT'S STILL STANDING!
EVEN AFTER ALL THE ATTACKS FROM QUEEN CHRYSALIS, AND THE STORM KING, AND KING SOMBRA.
CAN YOU EVEN BELIEVE IT?!
SUNNY! NOW IS **NOT** THE TIME FOR FANPONYING.
THE CRYSTAL THIEF WAS CLEARLY CALLING US HERE, SO WE CAN ASSUME THIS IS A TRAP. WE NEED TO STAY VIGILANT.

LOOK FOR ANY SIGNS OF MOVEMENT. IN FRONT OF YOU, BEHIND YOU.

!
?
!!
!
WE NEED TO BE COMPLETELY AWARE OF OUR SURROUNDINGS. BECAUSE IF WE'RE NOT PAYING ATTENTION...

...WE COULD END UP IN BIG...
...TROUBLE.

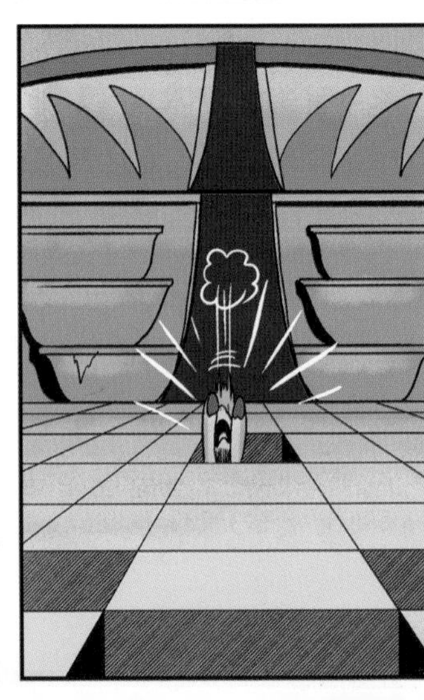

HOW CUTE IS THIS?!

SOMEPONY INVITED US TO A TEA PARTY! AND THESE DONUTS LOOK DELICIOUS! MAYBE NOT AS FINE A VINTAGE AS THE ONES EARLIER, BUT *C'EST LA VIE*--
I THINK THIS IS MORE OF A FILLY-NAPPING THAN A PARTY INVITATION, IZZY.

WOULD A FILLY-NAPPER HAVE MADE US HOMEMADE PLACE CARDS?
IZZY MOONBOW
REGINALD FURSOME IS THE ONE WHO MADE THOSE PLACE CARDS.

?!
KICK ME
?
MEEP.

REGINALD FURSOME

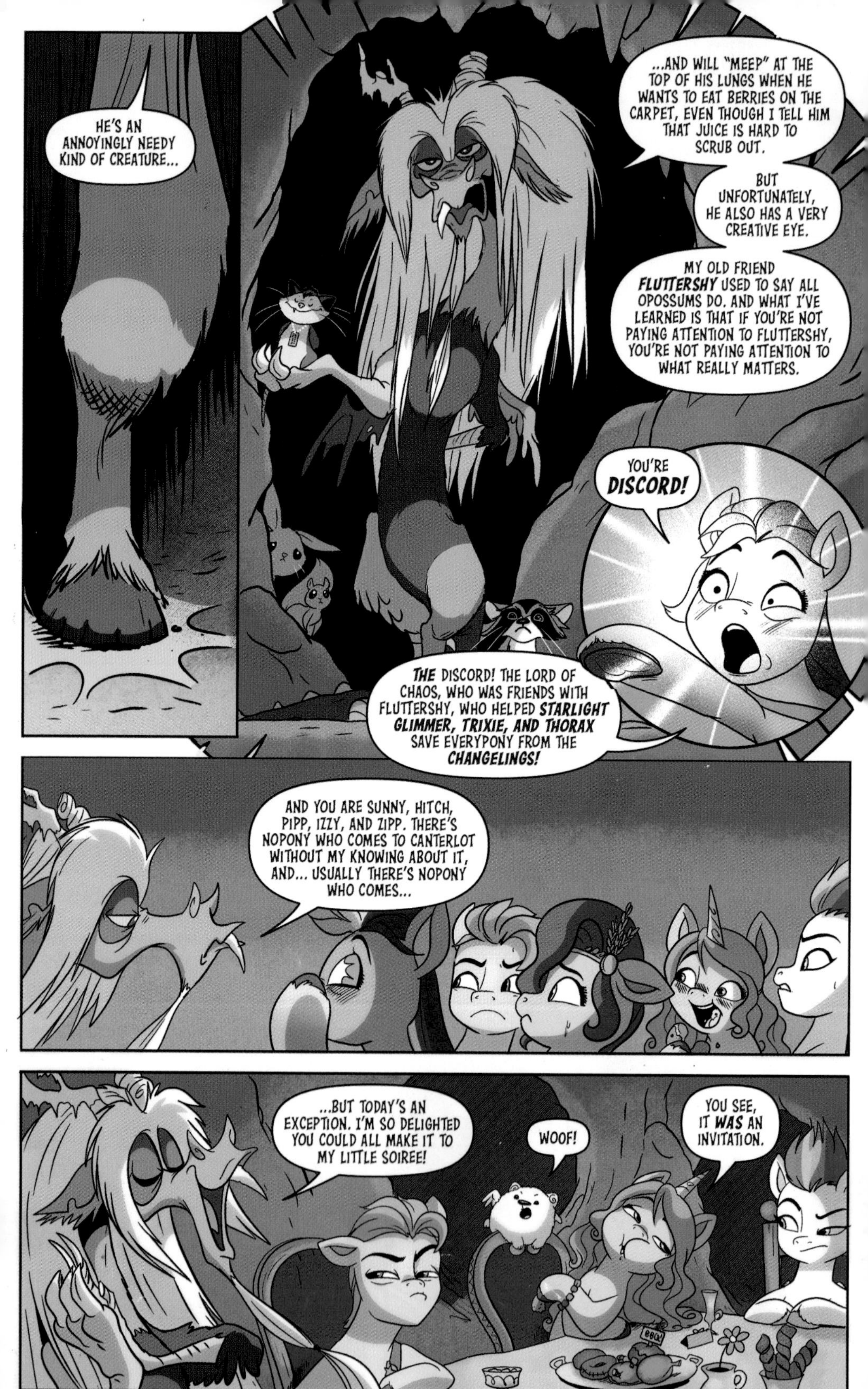
HE'S AN ANNOYINGLY NEEDY KIND OF CREATURE...
...AND WILL "MEEP" AT THE TOP OF HIS LUNGS WHEN HE WANTS TO EAT BERRIES ON THE CARPET, EVEN THOUGH I TELL HIM THAT JUICE IS HARD TO SCRUB OUT.
BUT UNFORTUNATELY, HE ALSO HAS A VERY CREATIVE EYE.
MY OLD FRIEND **FLUTTERSHY** USED TO SAY ALL OPOSSUMS DO. AND WHAT I'VE LEARNED IS THAT IF YOU'RE NOT PAYING ATTENTION TO FLUTTERSHY, YOU'RE NOT PAYING ATTENTION TO WHAT REALLY MATTERS.
YOU'RE **DISCORD!**
THE DISCORD! THE LORD OF CHAOS, WHO WAS FRIENDS WITH FLUTTERSHY, WHO HELPED **STARLIGHT GLIMMER, TRIXIE, AND THORAX** SAVE EVERYPONY FROM THE **CHANGELINGS!**
AND YOU ARE SUNNY, HITCH, PIPP, IZZY, AND ZIPP. THERE'S NOPONY WHO COMES TO CANTERLOT WITHOUT MY KNOWING ABOUT IT, AND... USUALLY THERE'S NOPONY WHO COMES...
...BUT TODAY'S AN EXCEPTION. I'M SO DELIGHTED YOU COULD ALL MAKE IT TO MY LITTLE SOIREE!
WOOF!
YOU SEE, IT **WAS** AN INVITATION.

MR. DISCORD, I HAVE SO MANY QUESTIONS FOR YOU--LIKE, **SO** MANY. BUT FIRST, WE REALLY NEED YOUR HELP.

ONE OF THE UNITY CRYSTALS WAS STOLEN. AND WE FOLLOWED THE THIEF HERE TO CANTERLOT. YOU WOULDN'T HAPPEN TO HAVE SEEN THE THIEF AROUND HERE, WOULD YOU?
SMOOTH.

THE THIEF IS EXACTLY WHY WE'RE HAVING THIS SOIREE! THERE IS SO MUCH TO TELL, AND IT ALL BEGINS WITH A DRAMATIC STORY.

THERE GOES MY MAGIC GLITCHING OUT AGAIN. STANDBY!

CRAK

HAS THAT STAGE BEEN THERE THE WHOLE TIME?
THAT LIGHTING IS COMPLETELY OVERSATURATING HIM. IT'S VERY UNFLATTERING.
ANYPONY WANT POPCORN?
HOOFBILL

"While age has been exceedingly kind to this handsome Lord of Chaos, many moons ago, when I was but a spry draconequus, I was part of a high-flying group."

IT WAS TWILIGHT SPARKLE, FLUTTERSHY, RARITY, PINKIE PIE, RAINBOW DASH, APPLEJACK, AND ME FIGHTING THE GOOD FIGHT.
OUR FANS CALLED US THE MANE-IFICENT 7.
THE HISTORY BOOKS MIGHT HAVE A FEW CORRECTIONS ON THAT ONE.
DID YOU JUST HAVE THAT SIGN READY TO GO?
Save your comments until the end, Sunny!
Yes. We did, Sunny.

"WE WERE QUITE THE HEROIC LITTLE TEAM, BUT TRUTH IS, WHEN TWILIGHT FIRST TOOK OVER AS RULER OF EQUESTRIA, THERE WASN'T MUCH FOR US TO DO.
"TWILIGHT MADE SURE EVERYPONY IN EQUESTRIA FELT RESPECTED AND CARED FOR, AND WE ALL LIVED IN-- WHAT'S THE OPPOSITE OF CHAOS? AH YES--
--HARMONY.
"DURING THOSE QUIET YEARS, FLUTTERSHY AND I CREATED AN ANIMAL SANCTUARY AND TOOK A FEW PROTÉGÉS UNDER OUR WINGS. WE TAUGHT THEM TO CARE FOR ALL THE CREATURES OF THE EVERFREE FOREST. IT WAS PURE AND UTTER BLISS.
"UNTIL A WICKED PONY CAME ALONG...
"...ONE WHO CAUSED PANDEMONIUM WITH HER FALSE IDEAS OF A PERFECT EQUESTRIA.
"THOSE WHO LISTENED TO HER STARTED BELIEVING SOME RACES OF PONY WERE BETTER THAN OTHERS SIMPLY BECAUSE OF THE MAGICAL ABILITIES THEY POSSESSED."
Flower
SO SORRY, BUT YOU NEED TO WAIT YOUR TURN LIKE EVERYPONY ELSE.
UNICORNS HAVE BETTER THINGS TO DO THAN WAIT IN LINE.

IT'S OKAY.
"BUT IT WAS FAR FROM OKAY.
"ONE INSTANCE LED TO ANOTHER, AND SOON PONYKIND FOUND THEMSELVES DIVIDED.
WATCH WHERE YOU'RE FLYING!
SORRY, YOUNG FELLA, BUT WE ONLY ALLOW EARTH PONIES INSIDE.
THESE PEGASI ARE ABSOLUTE HAZARDS.
"OUR FILLY PROTÉGÉS STOPPED ATTENDING OUR SESSIONS...
MY PARENTS SAY THERE'S NOTHING FOR ME TO LEARN FROM A LOWLY PEGASUS WHO CAN'T EVEN LEVITATE AN APPLE.
"IT WAS ALL VERY UPSETTING, BUT I KNEW I HAD TO HOLD IT TOGETHER FOR FLUTTERSHY."
SHE DIDN'T REALLY MEAN IT, DISCORD. HER PARENTS ARE JUST SCARED, THAT'S ALL.

"THEN TRULY TERRIBLE THINGS HAPPENED. MUCH OF WHICH IS FAR TOO FRIGHTFUL TO DESCRIBE. THINGS IN EQUESTRIA BECAME EVEN MORE DIVIDED.
"BUT FINALLY, AFTER MANY MOONS OF UNREST, THE MANE-IFICENT 7 WERE ABLE TO SET THINGS RIGHT.

"TO MAKE SURE MAGIC NEVER AGAIN PITTED UNICORNS, PEGASI, AND EARTH PONIES AGAINST ONE ANOTHER, TWILIGHT GATHERED ALL THE WORLD'S MAGIC AND PLACED IT IN THREE CRYSTALS.
"AS LONG AS THESE THREE CRYSTALS WERE PROTECTED, AND ALL PONYKIND LIVED IN HARMONY, MAGIC WOULD BE KEPT ALIVE AND WELL IN EQUESTRIA."

SO IT WAS TWILIGHT, RAINBOW DASH, APPLEJACK, RARITY, PINKIE PIE, AND FLUTTERSHY WHO CREATED THE CRYSTALS...
DISCORD, YOU NEED TO HELP US GET THAT MISSING CRYSTAL BACK SO WE CAN KEEP MAGIC ALIVE AND PROTECT THEIR LEGACY.
Applause!

MY DEAR SUNNY, THAT'S NOT WHAT I WANTED YOU TO TAKE FROM MY STORY.
I TOLD IT TO YOU SO YOU MIGHT QUESTION IF A SOCIETY WITHOUT MAGIC MIGHT ACTUALLY BE A MORE PEACEFUL ONE.
WAIT.

YOU STOLE THE PEGASUS CRYSTAL.
WHEN YOU REUNITED THE CRYSTALS AND MAGIC WAS RESTORED, I PANICKED. I DIDN'T WANT PONYKIND TO TURN AGAINST ONE ANOTHER AGAIN, SO I JUST... TOOK IT.

STOLE IT.
AND WHAT EXACTLY ARE YOU PLANNING ON DOING WITH THE CRYSTAL NOW?
DON'T ANGER HIM.

I'M NOT SURE... THAT'S WHY YOU'RE ALL HERE! IT'S TOO BIG A DECISION FOR ONE LORD OF CHAOS TO MAKE ON HIS OWN.

THE ANSWER IS EASY. ACCEPTING WHAT MAKES PONIES UNIQUE AND SPARKLE IS WHAT CREATES UNITY. WE NEED TO **EMBRACE** EACH PONY'S MAGIC, NOT STRIP IT AWAY FROM THEM.
AGREED.
SAME HERE.
YOU GOT IT, SUNNY!

AND WHAT ABOUT YOU? YOU'VE BEEN QUIET, AND I WOULD VERY MUCH LIKE TO HEAR WHAT YOU THINK OF ALL THIS.

I AGREE WITH SUNNY. EVERYPONY SHOULD GET TO KEEP THEIR MAGIC.

YOU DON'T SEEM SO SURE ABOUT IT THOUGH. AND I CAN'T HELP BUT WONDER IF IT HAS SOMETHING TO DO WITH YOUR ARRIVAL IN CANTERLOT. I NOTICED THAT YOU CAME IN ON YOUR OWN.
OH, WELL THAT'S ONLY BECAUSE WE SPLIT UP SO SUNNY, ZIPP, AND PIPP COULD USE THEIR MAGIC TO FLY ABOVE THE TREES AND HITCH COULD USE HIS MAGIC WITH THE FOREST CRITTERS.

AND YOU GOT LEFT BEHIND.
IT WASN'T EXACTLY LIKE THAT...

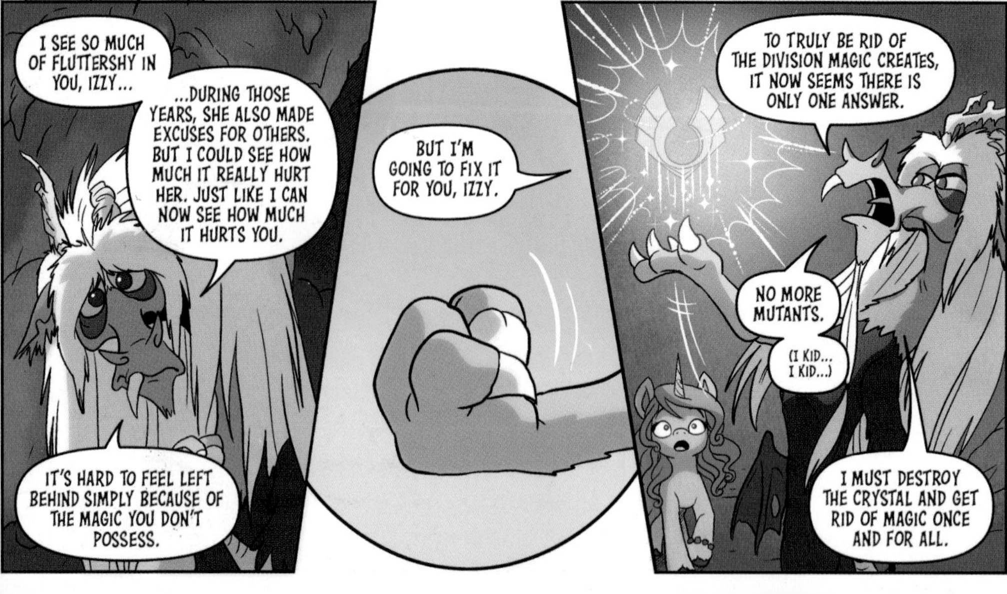
I SEE SO MUCH OF FLUTTERSHY IN YOU, IZZY...
...DURING THOSE YEARS, SHE ALSO MADE EXCUSES FOR OTHERS. BUT I COULD SEE HOW MUCH IT REALLY HURT HER. JUST LIKE I CAN NOW SEE HOW MUCH IT HURTS YOU.
IT'S HARD TO FEEL LEFT BEHIND SIMPLY BECAUSE OF THE MAGIC YOU DON'T POSSESS.
BUT I'M GOING TO FIX IT FOR YOU, IZZY.
TO TRULY BE RID OF THE DIVISION MAGIC CREATES, IT NOW SEEMS THERE IS ONLY ONE ANSWER.
NO MORE MUTANTS.
(I KID... I KID...)
I MUST DESTROY THE CRYSTAL AND GET RID OF MAGIC ONCE AND FOR ALL.

THAT'S NOT GOING TO HAPPEN ON OUR WATCH.
COME ON, PONIES. LET'S MAKE SURE THIS NUMBER'S A REAL SHOWSTOPPER.

YOU LOVE CANTERLOT HISTORY, SUNNY. LET ME TEACH YOU ABOUT CHAOS MAGIC!

SUNNY!
YOU LET HER GO, DISCORD.

UH-OH.

I'M STICKY. WHY DOES THIS KEEP HAPPENING TO ME?

ENOUGH OF THIS.
EVEN IF YOU WANTED TO DESTROY THE CRYSTAL, TWILIGHT'S MAGIC IS TOO POWERFUL. THERE'S NO WAY TO BREAK HER PROTECTIVE SPELL.
NO WAY THAT WE KNOW OF YET. BUT TWILIGHT TAUGHT ME THE POWER OF A LITTLE RESEARCH. I'M SURE I'LL FIGURE SOMETHING OUT.
THE THEATER CAN BE AN EMOTIONAL EXPERIENCE FOR EVERYPONY. YOU'VE BEEN A WONDERFUL--IF NOT ROWDY--AUDIENCE.

I HOPE WE REUNITE FOR ANOTHER TEA PARTY DURING MORE PEACEFUL TIMES.
SNAP

HE'S GOING TO FIGURE OUT HOW TO DESTROY THE CRYSTAL, AND IF WE DON'T STOP HIM IN TIME... WE'LL LOSE MAGIC FOREVER.
To Be Continued...

art by JustaSuta

art by Robin Easter

HOW ARE WE GOING TO STOP DISCORD IN TIME IF WE DON'T HAVE ANY CLUE WHERE HE COULD BE?
I COULD ASK MY PIPPSQUEAKS IF THEY'VE SEEN HIM.
WE DON'T WANT TO PANIC EVERYPONY. THERE'S GOT TO BE A BETTER WAY.

TOO BAD WE CAN'T TRACK HIS LUMINESCENCE. IT WAS ***TOTALLY*** GLITTERIFIC. LIKE A SUPER SHINY RAINBOW!

TRUE, BUT YOU MIGHT BE ONTO SOMETHING, IZZY. WE CAN TRY--

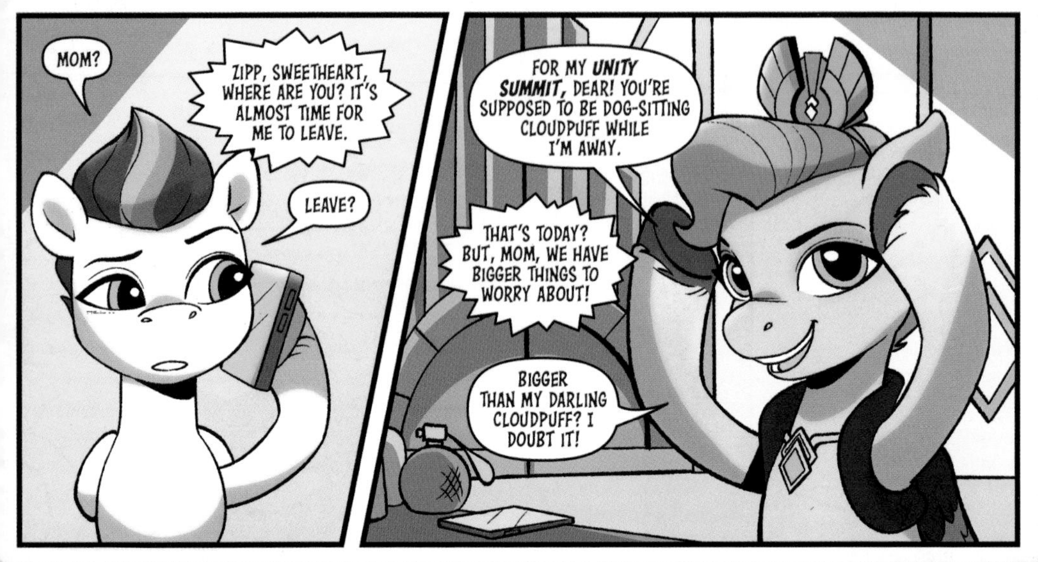
MOM?
ZIPP, SWEETHEART, WHERE ARE YOU? IT'S ALMOST TIME FOR ME TO LEAVE.
LEAVE?
FOR MY *UNITY SUMMIT*, DEAR! YOU'RE SUPPOSED TO BE DOG-SITTING CLOUDPUFF WHILE I'M AWAY.
THAT'S TODAY? BUT, MOM, WE HAVE BIGGER THINGS TO WORRY ABOUT!
BIGGER THAN MY DARLING CLOUDPUFF? I DOUBT IT!

I'LL SEE YOU SOON, DEAR! TOODLES!
CLIK
SO MUCH FOR INVESTIGATING. MOM IS PUTTING ME ON ROYAL DOG DUTY. I WANT TO HELP YOU PONIES SLEUTH THIS OUT, NOT PANDER TO A PRIZED POOCH.
THAT'S OKAY. THIS MEANS YOU CAN LOOK FOR LEADS IN ZEPHYR HEIGHTS! WE'LL HOLD DOWN THE FORT WHILE YOU'RE GONE.

GO FULFILL YOUR ROYAL DUTIES, **PRINCESS.** WE'VE GOT THIS.

...AND IF HE HASN'T HAD HIS BATH AND PAW MASSAGE BY EIGHT, HE GETS GRUMPY, SO MAKE SURE YOU'RE ON TIME.
YES, MOM.
YOU BE GOOD, ALL RIGHT? I'LL BE BACK TOMORROW EVENING.
PLOP
HAVE FUN, YOU TWO!

AND I MAY NOT BE ABLE TO TAKE YOU FOR AN "EVENING STROLL AROUND THE PROMENADE," BUUUUT...

HOW DO
YOU FIND A ROGUE
DRACONEQUUS WITH
NO LEADS?

AHA!
!

STOP RIGHT
THERE!
UH,
PRINCESS?
HORSEFEATHERS,
OF COURSE HE'S
NOT HERE.

HAVE YOU SEEN
ANYTHING...EXTRA
WEIRD LATELY?
SHAKE

ZIP
THANKS
ANYWAY!

COME ON, WEIRD CHAOS MAGIC, WHERE ARE YOU...
THIS IS IMPOSSIBLE, CLOUDPUFF. WE JUST GOT OUR MAGIC BACK. I DON'T WANT TO LOSE IT ALL OVER AGAIN.
I GUESS IT DOESN'T MATTER TO YOU. YOU'LL ALWAYS BE SPOILED, MAGIC OR NOT.
GOODNIGHT, CLOUDPUFF. ENJOY YOUR DINNER.

YAAWN

HEY, CLOUDPUFF. NOT TOO LONG UNTIL *YAWN* MOM GETS BACK.

HOW ABOUT YOU JOIN ME TODAY FOR-- HUH?

WHY DIDN'T YOU EAT YOUR DINNER, LITTLE GUY?

CLOUDPUFF?

GASP!

CLOUDPUFF? CLOUDPUFF! COME ON OUT, BUDDY!

THIS IS BAD! IF MOM CAN'T TRUST ME WITH PET DUTY, HOW WILL SHE TRUST ME WITH THE WHOLE KINGDOM?!

NO TIME TO FREAK. I JUST HAVE TO GET HIM BACK BEFORE MOM GETS HOME.

I JUST NEED A LITTLE HELP...
BBRING BBRRRING
NOW, SIR, WERE YOU AWARE YOU WERE GALLOPING IN A **TROT-ONLY ZONE?**

PARDON ME. SHERIFF HITCH TRAILBLAZER, AT YOUR SERVICE.

SHERIFF, I NEED SOME BACKUP. WE HAVE A CRITTER CAPER ON OUR HOOVES.
...ON MY WAY.

YOU'RE FREE TO GO... **THIS** TIME.

WHAT DID YOU CALL ME IN FOR? I THOUGHT **DETECTIVE ZIPP** WOULD WANT TO HANDLE THIS CASE ON HER OWN.
I HAVE A COUPLE OF IDEAS, BUT I WAS HOPING OUR LOCAL ANIMAL PSYCHIC MIGHT BE ABLE TO HELP ME NARROW IT DOWN.
BESIDES, EVERY GOOD DETECTIVE HAS A SIDEKICK.

I'M NOT **PSYCHIC.** ANIMALS JUST SPEAK TO ME. I'M ALSO NOT YOUR SIDEKICK.

LOOK--IF HE MISSED HIS DINNER, I BET HE'D TRY TO GET FOOD SOMEWHERE ELSE.

YOU'RE RIGHT! CLOUDPUFF IS A PICKY EATER, SO...

...HE'D GO SOMEWHERE WITH GOOD FOOD! I KNOW JUST THE PLACE.

Chez PEDIGREE
CLOUDPUFF? YES, 'E HAS A STANDING RESERVATION WITH US. CAME BY JUST LAST NIGHT.
REALLY? I MEAN--DO YOU KNOW WHERE HE WENT?
HM...
AH! I DO NOT KNOW FOR CERTAIN, BUT 'E AND QUEEN HAVEN OFTEN HEAD TO THE SHOPS ON RODEO AFTER LUNCH.
OF COURSE! THANK YOU, MR. PLATTER.

Chez PEDIGREE
YOU'VE BEEN A GREAT HELP, SIR.
GOOD LUCK, PRINCESS.

SEE ANYTHING?
NOPE. WAIT, MAYBE.

CLOUDPUFF APPROVED!
WELL THAT'S NEW.

RING
CLOSED

PRINCESS, HOW CAN I HELP YOU? WOULD YOU LIKE TO TRY OUR NEW OAT MASK?
Lavendar Balm's

NO, THANK YOU.
WE'RE ACTUALLY LOOKING FOR CLOUDPUFF. HAVE YOU SEEN HIM?

WHY, YES, THAT SWEET PUP MODELED FOR MY NEW LINE LAST NIGHT. IT'S A REAL BONUS TO HAVE THE ROYAL POOCH PROMOTING MY PRODUCTS, YA KNOW.

DID HE NOT GO BACK TO THE PALACE? I SENT HIM OFF WITH ONE OF MY PATENTED PERSONAL PAMPERING PACKAGES.

NO, HE DIDN'T.
DO YOU KNOW WHICH WAY HE WENT?
CLOSED

SHAKE

THE CITY GUARD MIGHT HAVE SEEN HIM ON HIS WAY OUT, BUT I'M AFRAID I CAN'T HELP.
CARE TO TRY SOME MANE OIL BEFORE YOU GO?

WE COULD ASK THE GUARDS, BUT WE'RE RUNNING OUT OF TIME. MOM WILL BE HOME SOON AND WE DON'T KNOW WHO WAS EVEN HERE WHEN CLOUDPUFF LEFT.
IT COULD HAVE BEEN ANYPONY.
OPEN

MAYBE WE DON'T NEED TO FIND ANY **PONY.**
!

?

COME ON. I KNOW HOW TO FIND OUR MISSING PUP!

THESE LITTLE GUYS SAY THEY KNOW WHERE CLOUDPUFF IS.

GOOD SLEUTHING, HITCH.

HEY, I'M SHERIFF FOR A REASON.
NOW, LET'S GO GET YOUR DOG BACK.

ALL RIGHT, LEAD ON, LITTLE BUDS!

ARE THEY SURE THEY KNOW WHERE WE'RE GOING? THIS IS A DEAD END.

THEY SAY THIS IS IT. SOMETHING ABOUT IT BEING A MATTER OF--

OOF

PERSPECTIVE! FROM PONY HEIGHT IT LOOKS LIKE A SOLID WALL, BUT FOR A CRITTER LIKE CLOUDPUFF IT'S CLEAR AS DAY.

YEAH, I DEFINITELY KNEW THAT.

SO WHERE IS--
HITCH, LOOK.

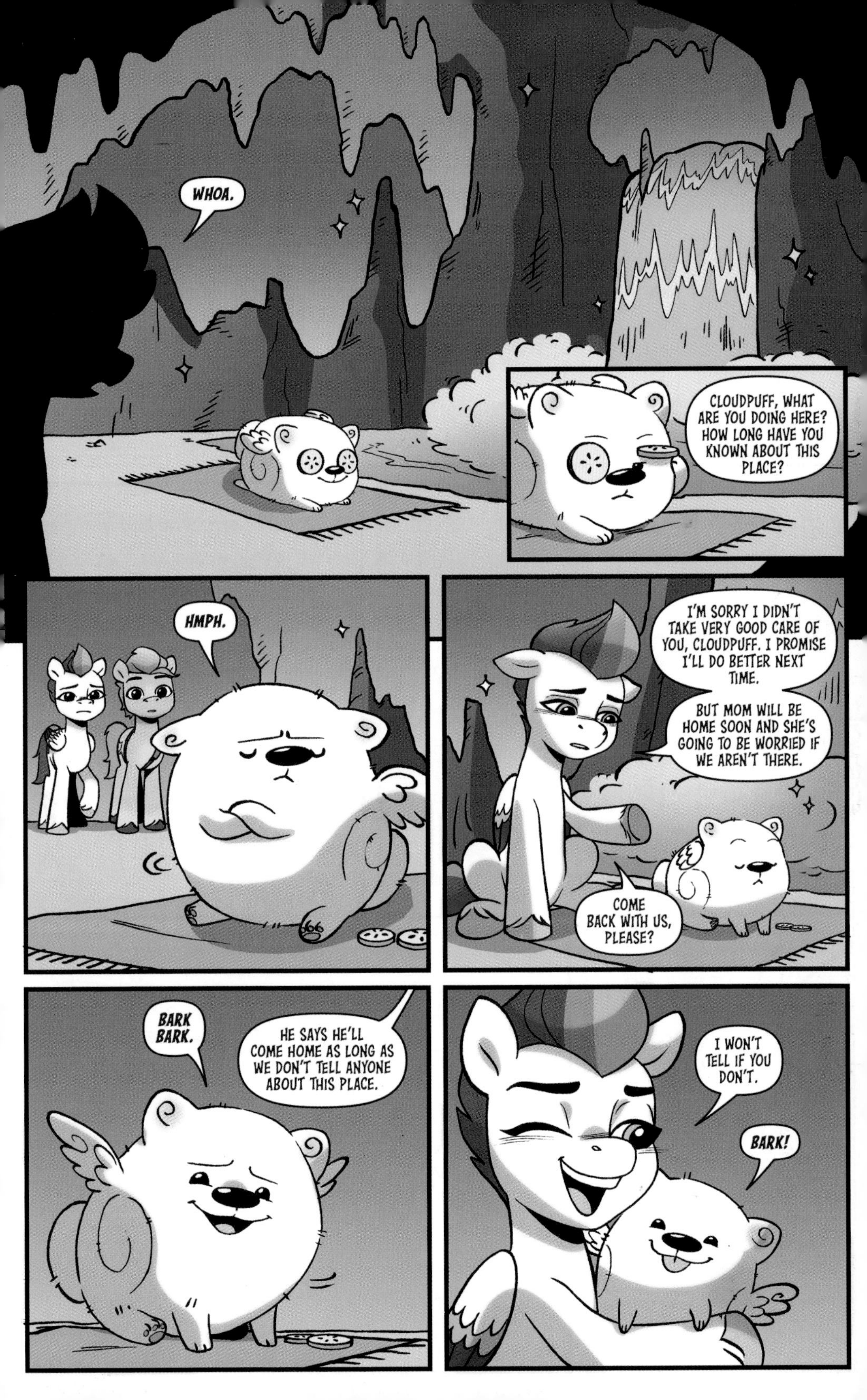
WHOA.
CLOUDPUFF, WHAT ARE YOU DOING HERE? HOW LONG HAVE YOU KNOWN ABOUT THIS PLACE?
HMPH.
I'M SORRY I DIDN'T TAKE VERY GOOD CARE OF YOU, CLOUDPUFF. I PROMISE I'LL DO BETTER NEXT TIME.
BUT MOM WILL BE HOME SOON AND SHE'S GOING TO BE WORRIED IF WE AREN'T THERE.
COME BACK WITH US, PLEASE?
BARK BARK.
HE SAYS HE'LL COME HOME AS LONG AS WE DON'T TELL ANYONE ABOUT THIS PLACE.
I WON'T TELL IF YOU DON'T.
BARK!

ZIPP, CLOUDPUFF! I'M HOME!

PHEW, WE MADE IT.

I MEAN... MOM! YOU'RE BACK! HOW WONDERFUL. WE WERE JUST--
GETTING SOME FRESH AIR!
YUP!

BARK BARK!

AWWW, DARLING! I'VE MISSED YOU TOO.

SWEETHEART, THANK YOU SO MUCH FOR WATCHING HIM. I HOPE HE DIDN'T GIVE YOU ANY TROUBLE.

TROUBLE? NO TROUBLE AT ALL.

WINK

HAS ANYONE HEARD FROM HITCH? HE WAS GOING TO HELP ME FOLLOW UP ON A POSSIBLE DISCORD SIGHTING, BUT I HAVEN'T SEEN HIM ALL DAY.

MAYBE ZIPP WILL KNOW! SHE'S SUPPOSED TO BE BACK SOON, RIGHT?

WAS SOMEONE ASKING ABOUT ME?

WOO, CALLED IT!
ZIPP! HITCH! WHAT WERE YOU TWO UP TO?

OH, YOU KNOW. DRAMA, ADVENTURE, MYSTERY!
NORMAL DOG-SITTING STUFF.

HA HA HA HA HA HA HA HA HA HA HA HA HA
WINK

art by JustaSuta

Pipp Gets Really Real

art by **Trish Forstner**

9:00
GOOOOOD MORNING, EVERYPONY! TODAY I'M TRYING SOMETHING A LITTLE DIFFERENT.
LIVE
INSTEAD OF STREAMING, I'VE DECIDED TO WRITE MY NEXT MAJOR LIFE UPDATE.
I KNOW, I KNOW! BUT THIS IS THE KIND OF UPDATE THAT CALLS FOR LOTS OF SELFIES.
LIVE
PLUS...
...IT'S ABOUT DISCORD.
OKAY, LOVE YOU, GOTTA GO WRITE! PIPP, PIPP, HOORAY!

GALLERY
9:00
PIPPSQUEAKS, WHEN I WENT FLYING WITH MY FRIENDS, I HAD NO IDEA IT WOULD LEAD TO A JOURNEY THAT ENDED IN DISCORD AND A UNITY CRYSTAL...
TAP TAP TAP
7:00
...AND THAT'S WHERE WE ARE NOW, SEARCHING FOR DISCORD BEFORE HE CAN DESTROY THE CRYSTAL! IF ANYPONY KNOWS HOW TO FIND HIM, WE NEED YOUR HELP! THANK YOU, LOVE YOU, PIPPSQUEAKS. PIPP, PIPP, HOORAY!
CLICK
POST
9:00
YAWN

9:05
100,157
99,398
6,780
MY LITTLE FILLY! HOW ARE THINGS IN THE BEAUTIFUL BRIGHTHOUSE?
GREAT!
UM, MOM? CAN I ASK YOU SOMETHING?
OF COURSE.
WELL, I'VE BEEN THINKING, MAYBE, ABOUT GETTING A LITTLE MORE ***REAL*** WITH THE PIPPSQUEAKS.
NO, THAT IS NOT FOR PETS!
SORRY, DARLING. "REAL" HOW?
I WANT TO WRITE ABOUT THE DAY EVERYPONY LEARNED I CAN'T FLY.
WHAT?!
BORK!

IT'S A LITTLE DIFFERENT FROM WHAT I USUALLY POST, BUT I THINK IT'S IMPORTANT.
BUT, DARLING, THAT DAY WAS SO HARD ON YOU.

IT WAS SUCH A DIFFICULT, CONFUSING, AWFUL DAY.
I WANT TO SHOW PEOPLE THAT SIDE OF ME.
THAT IT'S OKAY TO BE SAD SOMETIMES.

MMMP?
OF COURSE, MY BRAVE FILLY. IT'S A WONDERFUL THING TO DO.
BUT IF IT DOESN'T GO EXACTLY THE WAY YOU WANT IT TO, YOU'LL COME TELL ME, WON'T YOU? YOU KNOW YOU'RE ALWAYS WELCOME BACK HOME.
OF COURSE, MOM!
WHAT COULD GO WRONG?

TAPPITY TAP
DONE!
POST
SAV
MAYBE I SHOULD ASK MY FRIENDS WHAT THEY THINK BEFORE I POST IT.
CLICK
SAVE
YES, THAT'S A GOOD IDEA.
I'LL GET UP SUUUUPER EARLY AND ASK EVERYONE WHAT THEY THINK BEFORE THEY HEAD OUT FOR THE DAY.

12:00
12:00
12:00
OH NO! I OVERSLEPT!
EVERYPONY'S ALREADY GONE! I HAVE TO FIND THEM AND ASK ABOUT MY POST!

SUNNY! I KNEW YOU'D BE CLOSE BY. YOU'RE JUST WHO I WANTED TO TALK TO!
OH, HEY, PIPP. LATE NIGHT?
YES, I WAS... CREATING.
SUNNY, YOU'RE, LIKE, THE SMARTEST PONY I KNOW. I NEED YOUR ADVICE.
I WANT TO POST ON SOCIAL MEDIA ABOUT THE DAY EVERYPONY LEARNED I COULDN'T FLY. WHAT DO YOU THINK?
OH. THAT'S...
SORRY, PIPP. EVERYTHING WITH DISCORD HAS ME SO DISTRACTED. I CAN'T REALLY FOCUS ON ANYTHING ELSE.
OH. OKAY. I CAN ASK SOMEPONY ELSE.

WHY NOT TRY HITCH? HE'S WHO I GO TO WHEN I NEED A GROUNDED OPINION. UH, SO TO SPEAK.
THAT'S A GREAT IDEA!
HE'S IN THE MAIN SQUARE, I THINK, HELPING SET UP FOR THE STREET FAIR.
THANKS, SUNNY!

CAREFUL WITH THAT BANNER! WE DON'T WANNA BLOCK HOOF TRAFFIC!
...AGAIN.
HITCH! JUST THE PONY I WANTED TO SEE!
I AM?
YOU'RE SO SILLY SOMETIMES. YES!
I WANTED TO ASK YOU ABOUT MY NEXT BIG SOCIAL MEDIA POST!
RAISE THE BANNER MORE ON THE RIGHT SIDE!
UH... OKAY.
SORRY, PIPP, GO AHEAD.
I WANT TO POST ABOUT THE DAY EVERYPONY LEARNED I COULDN'T FLY. HOW SAD I WAS AND HOW ASHAMED I FELT.
WHAT DO YOU THINK?
ER, ISN'T THAT A LITTLE DIFFERENT FROM YOUR NORMAL POSTS? YOU KNOW, YOUR BRAND?
ISN'T IT USUALLY SINGING, SPARKLES, AND GLAMOUR?
YEAH, BUT THAT DOESN'T MEAN IT CAN'T CHANGE.
IT CAN BE SPARKLES AND REAL FEELINGS.
I SUPPOSE.
WELL, THANKS, I GUESS.
ANYTIME!
NO, NO, NO, THE BANNER'S ALL CROOKED NOW!

IZZY!
AGH!
IT TOOK ME FOREVER TO FIND YOU!
YEAH, I COME BACK TO WORK ON BIG CRAFTS PROJECTS. I FIND LA VILLA IZZY "CREATIVELY STIMULATING"!
THAT'S GREAT! BECAUSE I WANTED TO ASK FOR YOUR OPINION.
I WANT TO DO A SOCIAL MEDIA POST ABOUT WHEN EVERYPONY FOUND OUT ME, ZIPP, AND MY MOM LIED ABOUT BEING ABLE TO FLY.
WHAT DO YOU THINK?
UM...
THAT'S A GREAT IDEA!
REALLY?!
YES! IT'S JUST SO BRAVE!

BRAVE? WHY IS IT BRAVE?
I WOULD NEVER, EVER WANT TO TELL 1.6 MILLION PONIES ABOUT THE WORST, MOST EMBARRASSING, MOST HORRIBLE DAY OF MY LIFE!
OH, RIGHT. WELL I, UM, I SHOULD GO. BYE!
BYE, PIPP!
PIPP?
ZIPP! I NEED YOUR OPINION ABOUT MY SOCIAL MEDIA POST!
UMMM... OOOOKAY...
I WANT TO GET REALLY, REALLY *REAL* WITH MY FOLLOWERS.
I WANT TO TELL THEM ABOUT THE DAY EVERYPONY LEARNED WE COULDN'T FLY.
WHOA.
YES! I WANT TO SHOW EVERYPONY THAT IT'S OKAY TO FEEL SCARED OR HURT, LIKE I DID.

I MEAN, I THINK IT'S A GREAT IDEA, PIPP, BUT...
BUT WHAT?!
I DON'T KNOW, YOU USED TO WORRY A LOT ABOUT WHAT OTHER PEOPLE THOUGHT OF YOU.
I STILL DO! I MEAN, MY ONLINE PERSONA IS PART OF WHO I AM.
I KNOW, AND I'M AFRAID IF EVERYPONY DOESN'T RESPOND NICELY TO YOUR POST, YOU MIGHT TAKE IT PERSONALLY.
OF COURSE I WILL! IT'S EXTREMELY PERSONAL!
THAT'S MY POINT.
YOU KNOW I'M ALL FOR BEING YOURSELF, BUT MAYBE YOU SHOULD KEEP SOME DISTANCE BETWEEN YOU AND THE PIPPSQUEAKS, YOU KNOW?
I SUPPOSE I SEE WHAT YOU MEAN.
GOODNIGHT, ZIPP.
YOU TOO, PIPP.

POSTS - NEW - DRAFTS 1
INBOX
GROAN
CLICK
DRAFTS 1
CLICK
POST

Five minutes later.
48
27

One day later.
102
38

One week later.
BORK?
326
92

WHAT IS HAPPENING?!
BORK, BORK, BORK!

MY POST ABOUT DISCORD HAD OVER A HUNDRED THOUSAND VIEWS IN FIVE MINUTES! WHY DOESN'T ANYONE WANT TO READ THIS?!
BORK.

THAT'S IT! HITCH AND ZIPP WERE RIGHT! I'M DELETING IT.
TAP TAP
TAP TAP
DELETE

DING!
1

CLICK!
1

DEAR PIPP, MY NAME IS FELICITY. I'M A UNICORN, AND MY FAMILY JUST MOVED TO MARETIME BAY...

...I DIDN'T KNOW WHAT TO EXPECT. I'D NEVER EVEN SEEN THE OCEAN, AND I'D NEVER TALKED TO AN EARTH PONY.
I WASN'T SURE IF I WOULD FIT IN...

...OR IF I'D BE ABLE TO MAKE ANY FRIENDS.
I WAS SCARED IF I TRIED TO TALK TO THEM, THEY'D THINK I WAS BORING OR WEIRD.
SO I DECIDED TO MAKE THINGS UP.
I TOLD THEM ABOUT ME, MY FAMILY, AND BRIDLEWOOD.
BUT NONE OF THE STORIES I TOLD WERE TRUE.
I TOLD EVERYPONY THAT MY HOBBIES WERE SKYDIVING AND SURFING.
I SAID MY AUNT WAS A PRINCESS AND MY GRANDMA WAS A QUEEN.
I SAID I HAD TWO FULL-GROWN DRAGONS AS PETS AND A SPHINX WAS MY BEST FRIEND.
AT ONE POINT, I EVEN SAID BRIDLEWOOD WAS MADE OF COTTON CANDY.

EVERYPONY LOVED IT...
...BUT NONE OF IT WAS TRUE. I'VE NEVER SEEN THE OCEAN, I'M NOT ROYALTY, I DON'T KNOW ANY DRAGONS OR SPHINXES, BRIDLEWOOD IS MADE OF NORMAL TREES, AND I HATE, HATE, HATE HEIGHTS.
IT DIDN'T TAKE LONG FOR MY NEW FRIENDS TO FIGURE OUT I WAS LYING.
SOMEONE VISITED BRIDLEWOOD, AND, WELL, YOU KNOW WHAT I SAID ABOUT THE TREES.
EVERYONE WAS REALLY UPSET WITH ME, BUT THEY WEREN'T JUST ANGRY. THEY WERE HURT.
THEY SAID IF I'D TOLD THEM THE TRUTH, WE COULD'VE ALL STAYED FRIENDS.
BUT I HADN'T.
I'D BEEN AFRAID I COULDN'T MAKE FRIENDS, BUT THAT DAY, I FOUND OUT IT'S EVEN WORSE TO MAKE THEM AND LOSE THEM.

YOU MADE ME REALIZE I WASN'T ALONE, NOT REALLY. SOMETIMES WE LIE BECAUSE WE'RE SCARED THAT OUR FRIENDS WON'T ACCEPT US.

A wave of emotions hit me as everypony looked at me. I mean, I was right in the spotlight! Definitely not flying!

My face felt hot. I was so scared!

Then, later, I was sad. I'd deceived so many people I cared about. I'd never really thought it all through, but now that I was forced to, I knew I was wrong.

525 101
GOOOOOD MORNING, PIPPSQUEAKS. I WANTED TO TALK ABOUT A POST I RECENTLY PUT UP. MOST OF YOU PROBABLY HAVEN'T SEEN IT...

WHAT YOU'RE SEEING RIGHT NOW IS MY AUTHENTIC SELF, BEDHEAD-MANE AND ALL.
A LITTLE OVER A WEEK AGO, I SHOWED ANOTHER VERSION OF MY AUTHENTIC SELF.
PART OF ME IS THE BUBBLY PIPP WHO LOVES TO SING, DANCE, AND TALK TO ALL OF YOU.
BUT THERE'S ANOTHER PART OF ME. THE PIPP WHO'S SOMETIMES LONELY, SAD, AND AFRAID.
WHO MAKES MISTAKES.
LAST NIGHT, I WAS AFRAID THAT YOU WOULDN'T ACCEPT ME THE WAY I AM.
I THOUGHT, MAYBE I SHOULD DO A BETTER JOB OF HIDING IT.

SHOUT-OUT TO FELICITY FOR REMINDING ME THAT WHO I AM--EVERY PART OF ME--

oLIVE
--IS ENOUGH.
LOVE YOU, PIPPSQUEAKS. KEEP DOING WHAT YOU DO BEST: BEING YOU.

ALL OF YOU.
PIPP, PIPP, HOORAY!

1
New Message - From Discord

art by JustaSuta

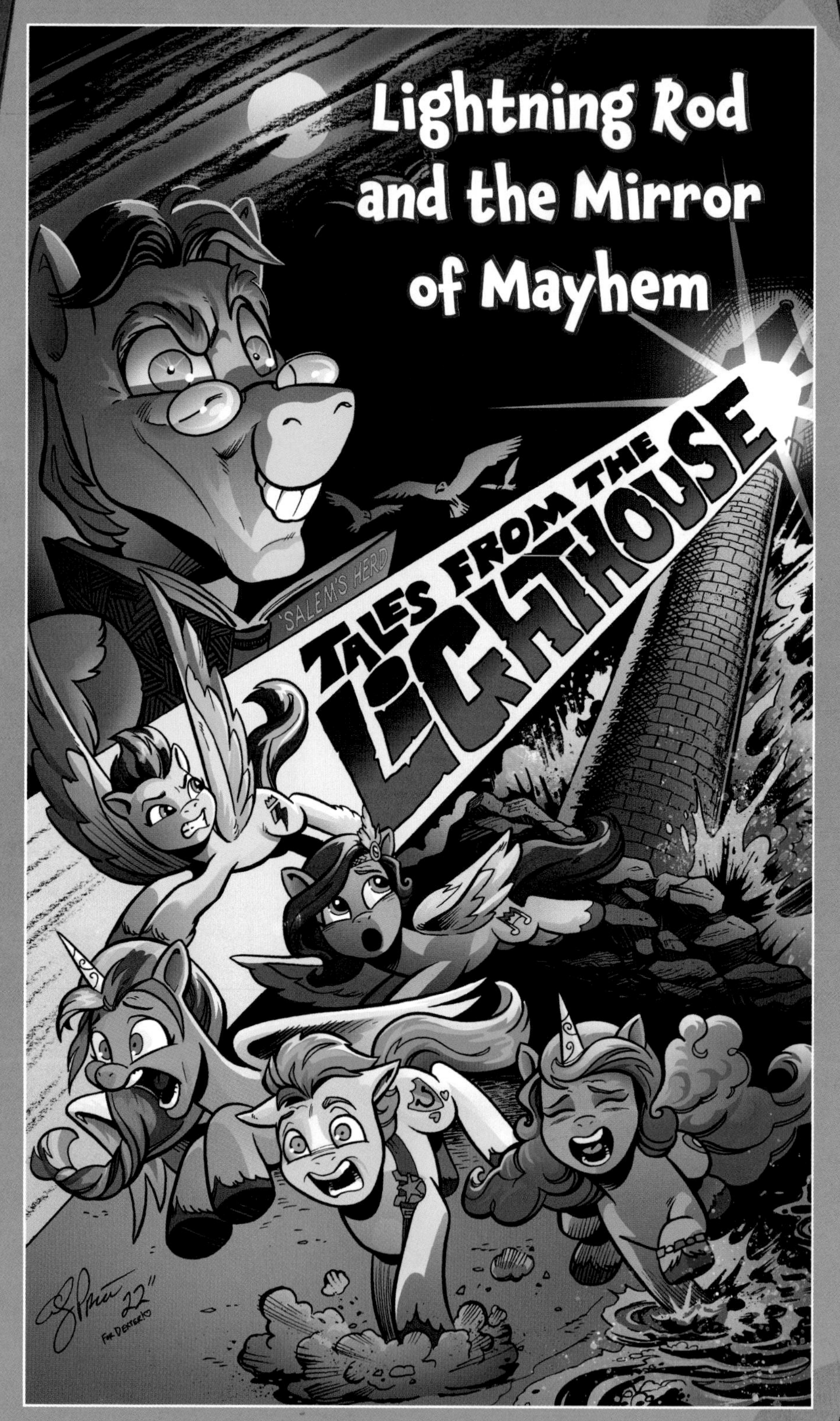

art by Andy Price

PIPPSQUEAKS, OUR SEARCH FOR DISCORD HAS BROUGHT US WAY OUT TO THE COAST. IF I DON'T CHECK IN SOON OR...
HEH.
...ANYTHING WEIRD HAPPENS, YOU KNOW WHERE TO FIND ME.
I HOPE!
PIPP, YOU MIGHT WANNA ADD A PSA* FOR YOUR FOLLOWERS.
IF YOU GET A MESSAGE INVITING YOU TO THE SCARIEST ABANDONED TOWN YOU'VE EVER SEEN FOR INFO ON A MISSING DRACONEQUUS...
...SAY YOU'RE BUSY THAT NIGHT.
IT'S FINE. C'MON, FOLLOW ME.
*PONY SERVICE ANNOUNCEMENT--ED.

SOMEPONY NEEDS TO KNOCK.
I'M FREEZING MY FLANKS OFF. DETECTIVE ZIPP?
I'M IN OBSERVATION MODE. PIPP? THIS WAS YOUR IDEA.
FOR HOOFNESS SAKE--
WELL NOW!
COME ON INSIDE. TAKE YOUR BOOTS OFF AN' LEAVE 'EM IN THE DOORYARD.
I'M SURE YOU'RE WONDERING WHY I ASKED YOU TO HAUL HOOF ALL THE WAY OUT HERE...
...TRUTH IS, I DON'T KNOW HOW ANYPONY USES THOSE GIZMOS. TOOK ME AGES TO WRITE THAT MESSAGE TO YA, PIPP.
Have some information on the whereabouts of a certain lord of chaos. Meet me.
Signed, A Friend
THANKS FOR SENDING IT-- WAIT! YOU NEVER TOLD US YOUR NAME!
I'M LIGHTNING ROD. AND THIS HERE'S THE WHISPERING BEACON, THE OLDEST LIGHTHOUSE IN EQUESTRIA. MOST EVERYPONY HAS FORGOTTEN WE'RE OUT HERE.
AYUP, EVERYTHING HERE IS LONG IN THE WITHERS, INCLUDING ME. BUT BEING AROUND A LONG TIME MEANS YOU HEAR THINGS.
THINGS ABOUT DISCORD?
HARD TELLIN' NOT KNOWIN', BUT MAYBE, JUST MAYBE, I KNOW A LEGEND THAT CAN GUIDE YOUR SHIP TO PORT, SO TO SPEAK.
TELL ME... WHAT DO YOU KNOW ABOUT CHAOS MAGIC?

CHAOS MAGIC
ACCORDING TO WIKIPONIA, CHAOS MAGIC WAS THE ENEMY OF THE ELEMENTS OF HARMONY, AND--
--WAIT, I COULD'VE READ THIS AT HOME AND SAVED MY MANE FROM SALT WATER DAMAGE. I WANNA KNOW WHAT **YOU** KNOW ABOUT CHAOS MAGIC.

YOU EVER HEAR ABOUT THE **MIRROR OF MAYHEM?**
DON'T BOTHA LOOKIN' 'EM UP ON YOUR PHONES. WON'T BE NOTHIN' THERE.
I DON'T THINK SO...
YOU SURE YOU'VE NEVER HEARD ABOUT THE BAD LUCK IT BRINGS? ABOUT THE TOWN IT DESTROYED?

SOMEPONIES SAY IT'S JUST A LEGEND, OTHERS SAY THE MIRROR IS CURSED, SOME SAY IT CAN CONTACT SPIRITS--
LIKE BLOODY MAREY?!
DON'T BELIEVE IN THAT NONSENSE. BUT I DO THINK...

SCARY STORY TIME!
WHAT DO YOU THINK, LIGHTNING ROD? WHAT'S BEHIND THE MIRROR OF MAYHEM?
I'M PRETTY SURE IT'S A CERTAIN **LORD OF CHAOS.**

Lightning Rod
and the
Mirror
of Mayhem

YE OLDE CURSES
"AS IT GOES, THE MIRROR OF MAYHEM MADE ITS WAY HERE BY SEA.
"NOPONY KNOWS WHERE IT CAME FROM, BUT WHEN THE SHIP PICKED UP THE CARGO HOLDIN' THE MIRROR...
"...THINGS GOT STOVE-UP REAL BAD.
"THEY SAY A PIRATE BY THE NAME OF CAPTAIN CANNON BONE KEPT THE MIRROR FOR HERSELF.
"AYUP, DIDN'T TURN OUT SO GOOD FOR HER, EITHER.

MORE CURSES

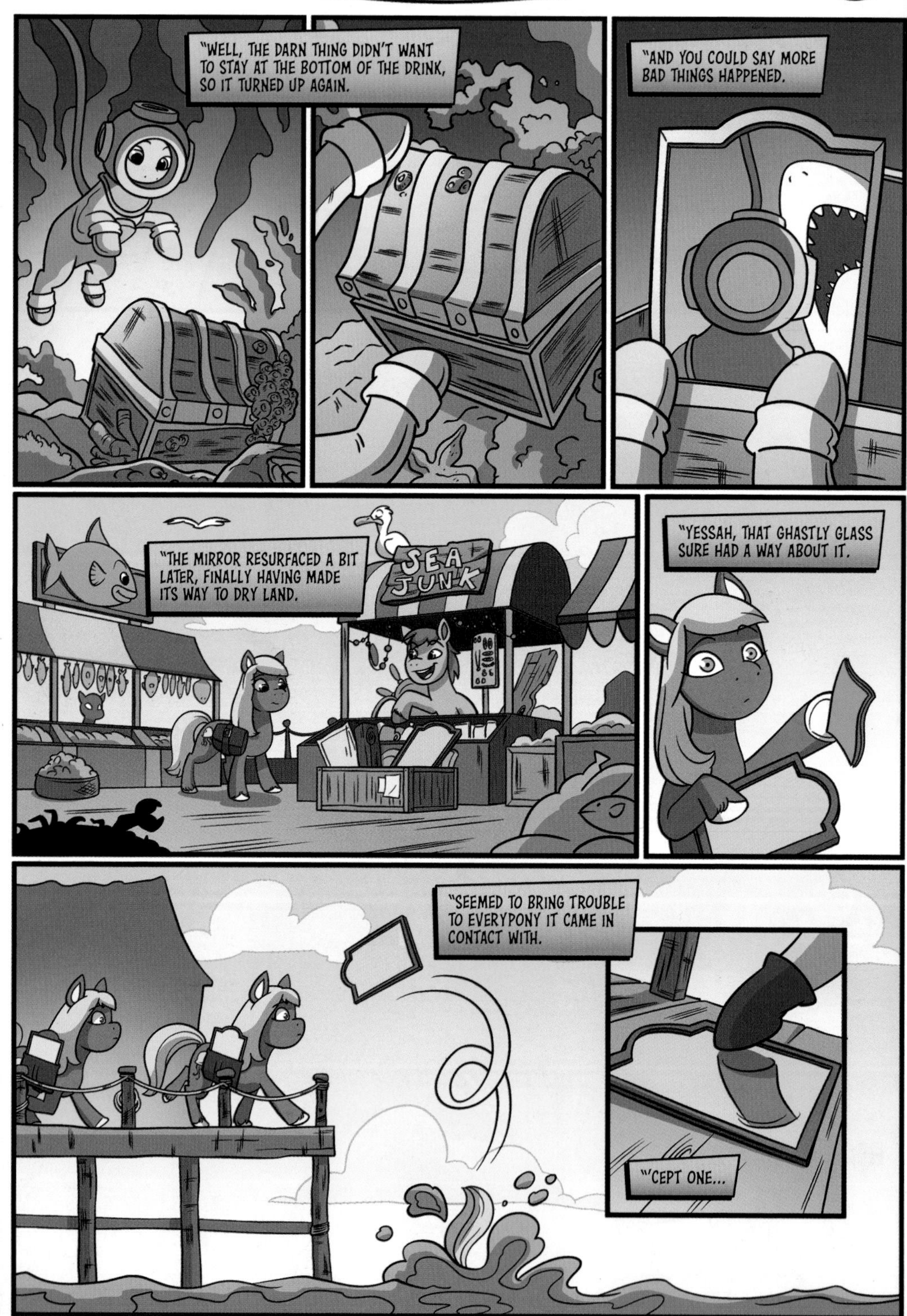
"WELL, THE DARN THING DIDN'T WANT TO STAY AT THE BOTTOM OF THE DRINK, SO IT TURNED UP AGAIN.
"AND YOU COULD SAY MORE BAD THINGS HAPPENED.
"THE MIRROR RESURFACED A BIT LATER, FINALLY HAVING MADE ITS WAY TO DRY LAND.
SEA JUNK
"YESSAH, THAT GHASTLY GLASS SURE HAD A WAY ABOUT IT.
"SEEMED TO BRING TROUBLE TO EVERYPONY IT CAME IN CONTACT WITH.
"'CEPT ONE...

"...FET LOCKLAND. USED TO BE ONE OF THE WEALTHIEST PONIES IN THESE PARTS. OPENED HIS SHOP RIGHT OVER IN CANDLEBRIGHT COVE.
OUTLAW ODDITIES
OUTLAW ODDITIES
"LOTSA YARNS ABOUT LOCKLAND, YESSAH. THEY SAID ALL HIS BITS CAME FROM CHAOS MAGIC.
"BUT HE DID EARN QUITE A BIT SELLING THE MIRROR.
"IN FACT...
"...HE SOLD IT A FEW TIMES.

YE OLDE LEGENDS
"WHERE EVERYPONY HAD NOTHING BUT ROTTEN LUCK, LOCKLAND DOWNRIGHT FLOURISHED.
OUTLAW ODDITIES
"STARTED CHARGIN' TO SEE THE MIRROR OF MAYHEM, AS HE CALLED IT.
"HE SAID..."
AYUP, JUST LOOK ON INTO THE MIRROR, SEE WHAT YOU'RE UPTA IN THE FUTURE.
"EVEN THOUGH THE CURSE SEEMED DORMANT...
"...THE MIRROR STILL MANAGED TO CAUSE GRIEF.
"AND MADE LOCKLAND VERY RICH.

GONE FISHING
"WHICH IS WHY EVERYPONY THOUGHT IT WAS SO **ODD** THAT HIS SHOP JUST CLOSED ONE DAY.

"BUT LOCKLAND HADN'T GONE ANYWHERE.
"AT LEAST, NOWHERE ANYPONY HAD GONE BEFORE.

"AND WHEREVER THAT WAS, IT SCARED FOLKS SOMETHIN' AWFUL."

WELL--
WELL?!

YOU CAN'T JUST LEAVE US HANGING LIKE THAT!
WHERE DID HE GO?
WHY ISN'T CANDLEBRIGHT COVE STILL AROUND?
WHAT DOES THIS HAVE TO DO WITH DISCORD?!
WAS FET LOCKLAND EVEN REAL?

AND MAY I *PLEASE* HAVE SOME MORE HOT CHOCOLATE?!
SOMEPONY CAN'T HOLD THEIR SUUUUGAR...

FIGURED I'D ANSWER THE EASY QUESTION FIRST.
ESPECIALLY CONSIDERING YOU WERE BUZZIN' AROUND HERE LIKE A BEE IN A MITTEN.
HA. I'M SORT OF A DETECTIVE, AND WHEN I CAN'T CRACK A CASE, I JUST GET A LITTLE...
TELL ME WHO, TELL ME WHERE, TELL ME NOOOW!
OH, FOR HOOFNESS SAKE! OKAY, OKAY, I'LL CHILL.
BUT WE STILL DO NEED TO KNOW ABOUT DISCORD!
AS I WAS SAYING...
...THIS IS WHERE THINGS GET COMPLICATED.
THINGS GET MORE COMPLICATED?
AYUP.

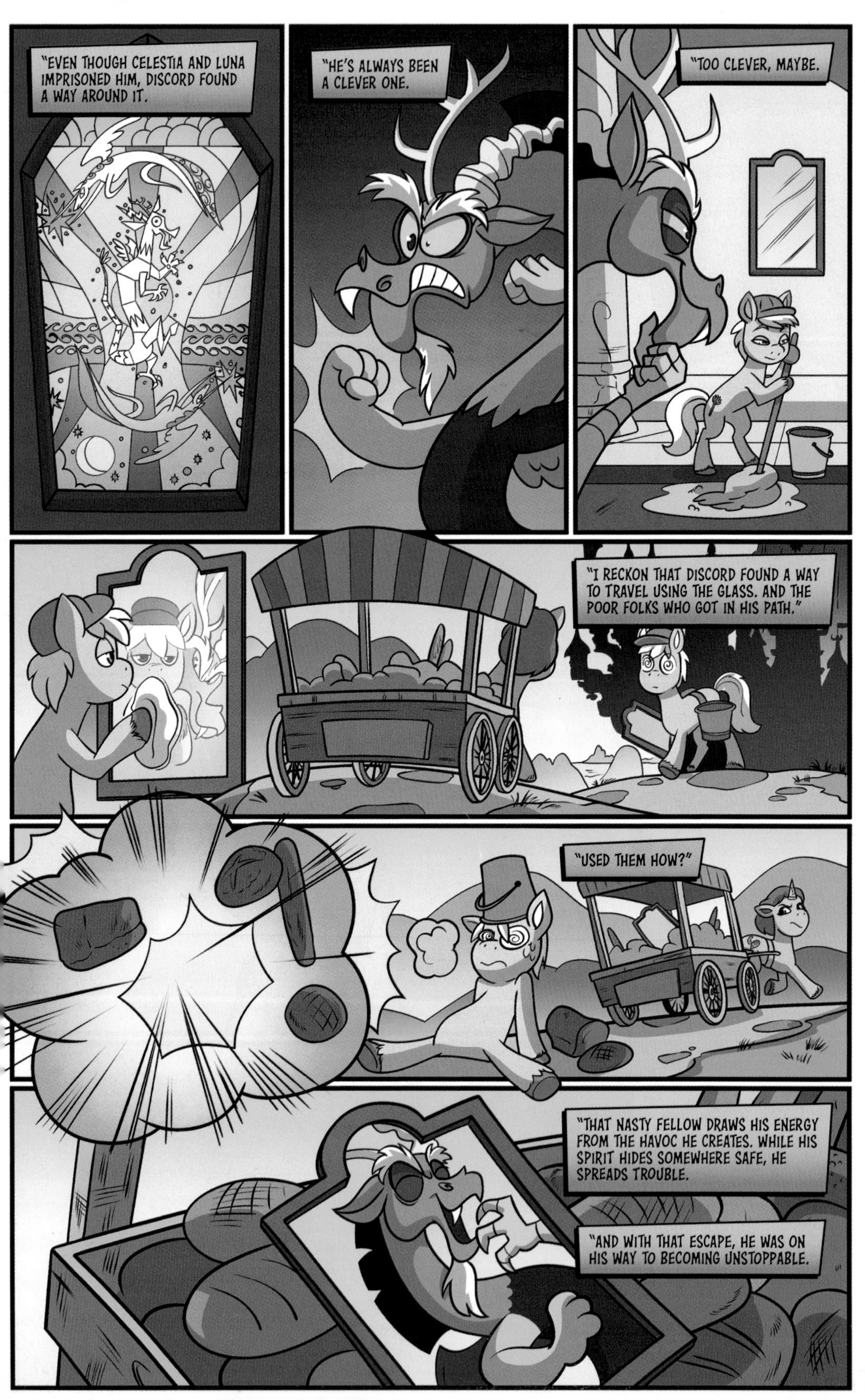
"EVEN THOUGH CELESTIA AND LUNA IMPRISONED HIM, DISCORD FOUND A WAY AROUND IT.
"HE'S ALWAYS BEEN A CLEVER ONE.
"TOO CLEVER, MAYBE.
"I RECKON THAT DISCORD FOUND A WAY TO TRAVEL USING THE GLASS. AND THE POOR FOLKS WHO GOT IN HIS PATH."
"USED THEM HOW?"
"THAT NASTY FELLOW DRAWS HIS ENERGY FROM THE HAVOC HE CREATES. WHILE HIS SPIRIT HIDES SOMEWHERE SAFE, HE SPREADS TROUBLE.
"AND WITH THAT ESCAPE, HE WAS ON HIS WAY TO BECOMING UNSTOPPABLE.

"HE MADE HIS WAY HERE.
"MAYBE HE SENSED FET'S MAGIC...
"...AND TOOK THOSE POWERS FOR HIMSELF.
"EVENTUALLY, THE SHOP WAS CLEANED OUT, AND FOLKS WENT ON WITH THEIR LIVES.
OUTLAW ODDITIES
"BUT DISCORD WAS STILL WAITING...
"...FOR SOME NAIVE FOOL TO COME ALONG."

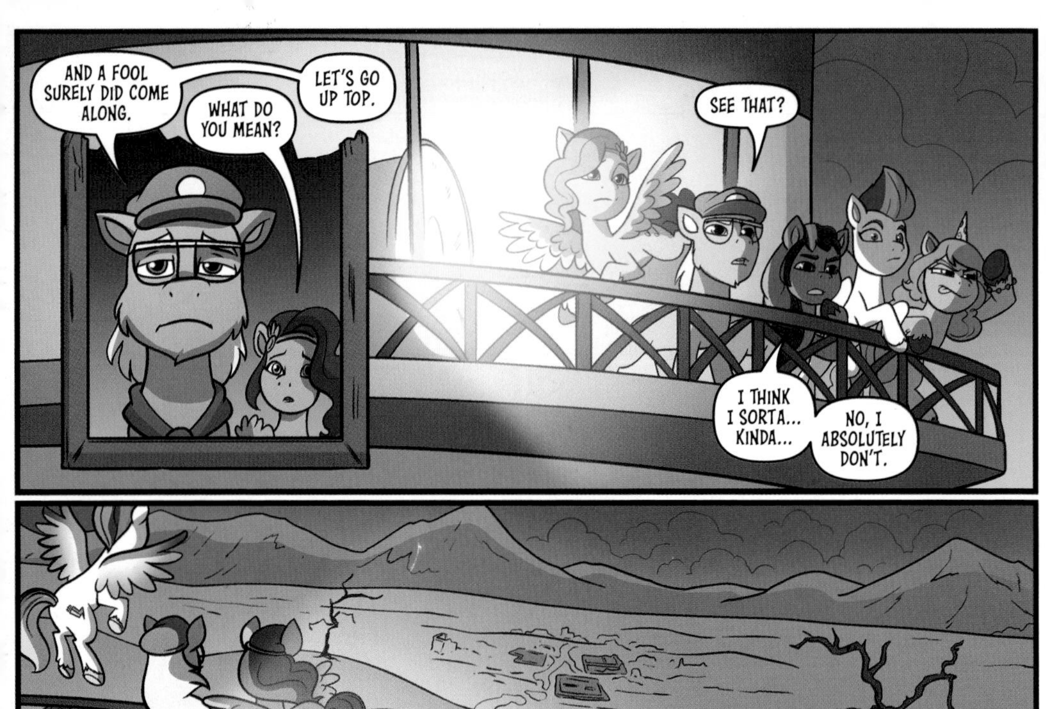
AND A FOOL SURELY DID COME ALONG.
WHAT DO YOU MEAN?
LET'S GO UP TOP.
SEE THAT?
I THINK I SORTA... KINDA...
NO, I ABSOLUTELY DON'T.

THAT USED TO BE CANDLEBRIGHT COVE.

WHAT HAPPENED TO IT?
ME.
WE'RE GONNA NEED MORE HOT CHOCOLATE FOR THIS. AND MAYBE SOME SNACKS.
FOLLOW ME.

I KNEW WHEN I SENT THAT EMAIL THAT I WAS READY TO COME CLEAN, BUT--
DO YOU MIND IF I JUST... Y'KNOW...
I'M ALL MUGUP FROM THE HOT COCOA, BUT HELP YOURSELF.
THESE PHOTOS ARE FROM JUST BEFORE... WELL, SEE FOR YOURSELVES.
"CANDLEBRIGHT COVE WAS A REAL NICE TOWN. I HAD GOOD FRIENDS, DID AN IMPORTANT JOB, FELT LIKE PART OF THE COMMUNITY.
"BACK THEN, BEIN' A KEEPER WAS A BIG DEAL.
"BUT THINGS CHANGED. THINGS ALWAYS CHANGE."
EXCEPT ZIPP.
THE PIPPSQUEAKS ARE GOING TO LOVE THIS, ESPECIALLY IF SHE DROPS IT!
YOU READY FOR ONE LAST SCARY STORY?

"I CAME TO CANDLEBRIGHT COVE BECAUSE THEY DIDN'T MIND MAGIC, UNLIKE SOME OTHER PLACES.
"THIS HARBOR USED TO BE A MAIN PORT, YESSAH. LED LOTS OF BOATS TO SHORE, HELPED LOTS OF FOLKS.
"OVER THE YEARS, CANDLEBRIGHT COVE GREW. GOT MORE MODERN.
"AND THEN...
"...I'D HAD THE THING FOR YEARS, NOTHING BAD HAD EVER HAPPENED. UNTIL THAT DAY IN MY LIGHTHOUSE."
YESSS, YOUR LIGHTHOUSE...
"I SHOULD JUST USE MY POWERS, HE SAID. THEY'D HELP FREE HIM.
"SURELY THERE MUST BE ANOTHER WAY, I ASKED HIM.
"IF IT WAS MY POWERS HE WANTED, WELL, I WAS GONNA MAKE SURE HE GOT 'EM.
"IT WAS LIKE THE TOWN HAD NEVER EXISTED.
"I NEVER MEANT-- I THOUGHT I'D JUST DESTROY THE MIRROR.

"TECHNOLOGY MEANT BOATS WERE GUIDED DIFFERENTLY, DIDN'T NEED AN OLD LIGHTHOUSE ANYMORE.
"OR THE KEEPER.
"I DECIDED IT WAS TIME TO MOVE DOWN THE ROAD APIECE. DIDN'T WANT TO STICK AROUND TO WATCH MYSELF BECOME OBSOLETE.
"HE SAID HE'D MAKE SURE THE TOWN ALWAYS NEEDED ME, THAT I'D ALWAYS HAVE A HOME.
"WHAT HE WANTED IN EXCHANGE, THOUGH...
"IMAGINE THE CHAOS IF JUST A FEW BOATS RAN UP SHORE, HE SAID.
"I SHOULD JUST USE MY POWERS, HE SAID. THEY'D HELP FREE HIM.
KABOOM
"WHAT WAS LEFT OF IT SHOWS SOME THINGS, BUT WITH THAT PIECE BROKEN... WELL, DISCORD WAS GONE."

THAT'S MY STORY. AND THAT'S WHY I ASKED YOU OUT HERE.
THAT WAS VERY BRAVE OF YOU. IT MUST'VE BEEN SO HARD.
WHAT WOULDA BEEN BRAVE WAS LETTING THE TOWN GROW, LETTING THINGS CHANGE.
INSTEAD I HELD ON TO THE PAST AND ENDED UP ALONE. BUT AT LEAST THE MIRROR ISN'T HURTING ANYPONY ANYMORE.
CHANGE! THAT'S IT!
DISCORD DOESN'T WANT ANYTHING TO CHANGE. I BET HE STILL USES THE SAME HIDEOUT HE DID BACK THEN! WE CAN JUST LOOK IN THE MIRROR--
I FORGOT, IT'S BROKEN. YOU REALLY CAN'T SEE WHERE HE'S AT, LIGHTNING ROD?
NO, NO, YOU CAN'T SEE THERE FROM HERE WITH IT BROKEN. BUT...

...THE OTHER PIECE IS OUT WHERE THE TOWN USED TO BE, PROBABLY BURIED UNDER THE RUBBLE.
WHEN I SAW YOUR MESSAGE, I KNEW IT WAS TIME TO FINALLY DO SOME OF THE GOOD I MEANT TO.

WE CAN REALLY FIND HIM WITH THIS, CAN'T WE?
WE CAN STILL SAVE MAGIC.

YOU'VE BEEN KEEPING THIS SAFE FOR SO LONG. LIKE, AS I DO THE MATH, AN EXCEPTIONALLY LONG TIME.
ARE YOU GONNA BE OKAY WITHOUT IT?
OH, I THINK IT'S WELL PAST TIME FOR ME TO FIND A NEW HOBBY.
MAYBE I'LL TRY BLOGGING, LIKE YOU.
THANKS FOR REMINDING ME! CAN WE GET A SELFIE? Y'KNOW, FOR MY NEXT UPDATE.
WHEN EXACTLY DID ALL THIS START? IT DOES SEEM LIKE YOU'VE BEEN HERE A REALLY, REALLY, REEEEEALLY LONG TIME...
...SOMETHING ISN'T ADDING UP.
ZIPP! YOU SAID YOU'D CHILL!
THANK YOU ALL. FOR LISTENING. FOR HELPING ME PUT THINGS RIGHT.
WE'LL LET YOU KNOW HOW IT GOES.

WOW, I MEAN, **WOW!** CAN YOU BELIEVE THAT?
NOT REALLY, NO. I BELIEVE THE STORY, BUT I HAVE SO MANY QUESTIONS.
HOW DOES HE GET CELL SERVICE OUT HERE? WHERE DOES HE GO GROCERY SHOPPING? THIS PLACE IS DESOLATE!
WHY DIDN'T HE JUST GIVE US THE MIRROR TO BEGIN WITH? WHY TELL US--
ZIPP, IF I'VE LEARNED ANYTHING FROM STREAMING...
...LIGHTNING ROD IS A NATURAL CONTENT CREATOR. **EVERYPONY** LOVES A STORY. EVERYPONY LOVES A LITTLE MYSTERY.
UH...
I SAID A **LITTLE!**
DID SOMEPONY REQUEST A MYSTERY?
TO Be CONTINUeD...

art by JustaSuta

art by Brianna Garcia

art by **Amy Mebberson**

art by JustaSuta

art by Trish Forstner

art by Trish Forstner

art by Konrad Kachel

art by Trish Forstner

art by Mike Federali

art by Nicoletta Baldari